P9-DEV-028

MOISE AND THE

WORLD OF REASON

by *Tennessee Williams*

SIMON AND SCHUSTER • NEW YORK

COPYRIGHT © 1975 BY TENNESSEE WILLIAMS
ALL RIGHTS RESERVED
INCLUDING THE RIGHT OF REPRODUCTION
IN WHOLE OR IN PART IN ANY FORM
PUBLISHED BY SIMON AND SCHUSTER
ROCKEFELLER CENTER, 630 FIFTH AVENUE
NEW YORK, NEW YORK 10020

DESIGNED BY IRVING PERKINS
MANUFACTURED IN THE UNITED STATES OF AMERICA
BY AMERICAN BOOK—STRATFORD PRESS, INC.

2 3 4 5 6 7 8 9 10

LIBRARY OF CONGRESS CATALOGING IN PUBLICATION DATA

WILLIAMS, TENNESSEE, 1911–
   MOISE AND THE WORLD OF REASON.

   I.   TITLE.
PZ3.W67655MO [PS3545.I5365] 813'.5'4 74-31061
ISBN 0-671-21982-0 REGULAR
ISBN 0-671-22066-7 DELUXE

FOR ROBERT

The white blackbird exists, but it is so white that it cannot be seen, and the black blackbird is only its shadow.

—JULES RENARD

I

THIS ROOM of Charlie's and mine wasn't really a room, it was a small section of an abandoned warehouse near the South Hudson docks. It was graced with a minimal sort of lavatory and a precipitous flight of stairs to West Eleventh Street and it was scantily partitioned off from the vastness in which it crouched by three walls of plywood which ascended about halfway to the ceiling. Sometimes I called it "the rectangle with hooks," for an earlier lover of mine, the only earlier lover, had placed hooks in the plywood to hang things on, and at the risk of committing a pathetic fallacy, I will add that there was not much to hang on them anymore.

But I am not a materialistic person as most sensualists are. I am a very sensual person. I suppose I would have to confess that I am, it is so apparent in my writing, both in the truths and the fantasies of my existence, and I think it is visible in my eyes, as visible as a thing printed in primary colors in public view. Of course as one grows older, and I am now more than twice the age at which I met my first love, there is a tendency to put on some materialism, probably through exposure to it in others. At the age of fifteen, when I met my first love, Lance, and committed my life to his, I was already a sensualist but material things were of little consequence to me, and I don't believe that I expressed any surprise when he introduced me to his living quarters, astonishing as they were. Well, I'm a Southerner from a small town and it's traditional among those of such origin to be politely silent about whatever oddities they observe in the life styles and mannerisms of those who entertain them. I suppose if we're offered a slice of cake or cup of coffee and discover a bug in it, well, we may not pretend to eat or drink it but we don't like to say, "There's a bug in this," we just sort of shove it slightly aside as if more interested in the individual than in the "refreshments" offered. I may have looked at Lance with a hint of something that was like a question, the first night that he introduced me to the hooked rectangle, for he sat right down on the clean, well-made bed, somewhere between single and double, accommodating two bodies with ease provided that they loved without reserve, and he grinned at me and said, "Baby, this is better than the streets but not much better, I know that."

My response was a delighted comment on the clothes, professional and social, that were suspended from the hooks about the rectangle. They were "elegant funk," I guess that's their definition, and inclined to glitter, designed for a glamorous night life, either far uptown or downtown.

He looked at me seriously then, and said, "Baby, let's not delude yourself about it. All this paraphernalia, these glittery costumes on the hooks, can't possibly blind you to the fact that this ain't a suite at the Waldorf, and I better explain to you right now that the circumstances I live in are not so much adapted to the way I live now as the way that I may have to live in the future."

I smiled and said, "I see," although what he meant was far beyond my conjecture that first night.

So much, and maybe too much, about how I came to live here. As a writer I don't concentrate on craftsmanship: still I know, intuitively, when a piece of explication should be extended no further than the point at which it can be dropped.

Now I have informed you that I am a writer and a reasonably young writer, at least in the number of my years on earth, but you've probably also surmised that I am a failed one, which is the indisputable truth. My writing desk was a wooden box with the fading words BON AMI printed on it. The light bulb was long extinct and no one had cared to replace it. There were windows on this floor of the warehouse but not in our section of it and two of them nearby had been shattered by a storm so that there was no way to keep the elements out, but when the human element of love is present, even in such a drab and restricted space, the elements outside are of relatively small consequence most of the time, and if you don't know that to be God's truth, then you've never lived with a fellow being like Charlie in your lifetime, nor with the other love to whom I've alluded.

Oh, I've neglected to mention that that previous love of my life, a light-skinned black, skater by profession, who referred to himself as "the living nigger on ice," had honored my twenty-first birthday with a record player with records by Ida Cox, Bessie Smith and by Billie Holiday, the third an idol whose habits he emulated too closely. To this original collection of records there had been no addition till a month ago when the proprietor of the bar nearby changed the records on his music box and presented me with my favorite, a haunting pop number called "Killing Me Softly with His Song." This record player is right by the bed and that new record is always on it. I always turn it on just before getting into bed and Charlie makes fun of me for being moved to tears by it as I once was moved to tears by Lady Day singing "Violets for Your Furs."

Charlie says that my undoing as a writer is an excess of sentiment and that's a point I've never argued with him, not even so much as to say, "Baby, you're twenty and I'm thirty and you'll abandon me some day or night more thoroughly than this old warehouse has been abandoned." Perhaps I ought to say something like that to Charlie, but I suspect he would laugh, not to dismiss the idea but at the Bavarian burgher that still runs in my blood as a heritage from my father's forebears.

Time now to begin with yesterday afternoon.

Charlie and I were reluctant to get out of bed as it was the bitterest day of the winter. Charlie had the flu in its early feverish stage which made his body deliciously warm to touch. The thought of racing naked to the bathroom was a shivering thought that nevertheless had to be entertained since it was now half past four and we had promised Moise to help her prepare for her mysterious party which was supposed to start at five-thirty. I know that Moise is a strange name to introduce so abruptly but that's her name. It is her first, last and only name as far as anyone I know or have known seems to know. It does not rhyme with noise. It rhymes with nothing I know and since, as this Blue Jay continues, you will encounter the name again and again, let me pronounce it for you. Say *mo*. And then say *ease*, with the accent placed (ironically) on the ease. And as for the rest of the name that I'll give to this work, you will soon come to see not only the relevance but the final necessity of it, there being, among the universal dualities, among the pluralities, always the world of reason and that which is outside it: enough about that for now.

It's time to return to yesterday afternoon.

Charlie tried to tell me that the one-legged nickel-plated clock on the box by the bed had stopped during the night but I held it to his ear so he could hear it was ticking. Then he tried to detain me by further love play but I said, "Baby, save it," and rushed into the improvised bathroom and before I'd finished peeing he joined me over the cracked seatless bowl and it was good to be in contact again with his little heating apparatus of a body. I'd got it down and it started up again now, if you know what I mean, which I know is a stupid question, and I thought it was a little far out even for a kid from the cattle-land of Texas when he did this thing which is probably too far out for me to report but seems to demand inclusion in the scene. He caught the stream of my pee in his cupped hands and then rubbed it over his face as if he were applying after-shave lotion to it, and, yes, it was a touch of intimacy that I, who was his senior by ten years and not from the cattle-land of Texas, felt obliged to put down.

"Let's not get into that sort of thing," I said to him sharply. But he smiled up at me, so bright and innocent with his teeth chattering that I laughed and slapped his ass lovingly and turned on the washbowl that only ran water so cold that it was a wonder that it was able to run.

And it was so cold in the room that we didn't stop to consider what to put on for Moise's party. We just jerked into the clothes we'd dropped by the bed the night before.

"Moise will be unhappy that we didn't dress up," said Charlie.

"I doubt that she'll notice. Put your sweater on and my muffler and army jacket."

"Yes, Mother." For once he was eager to comply with a suggestion of mine as nothing he put on would be enough to be comfortable inside or outside of.

"Uninhabitable quarters!" I said with a glance around me. And now already I am indulging in the fractured sentence which is the stylistic practice in my writing which has been most irritating to the editors of the few publications to which I've submitted my work.

"Yes, now let's get cracking!"

But I had to wait a minute at the stair-top while he fooled with his shoulder-length red-gold hair, saying from behind the plywood, "I think it's getting too long for anything but a ponytail, don't you?"

"Fuck your hair."

"Why not?" he laughed. "I guess it's all that you haven't."

And now we were running downstairs and our breath whistling between our teeth steamed like horses' breath before we got out the door.

"Why is Moise giving this party?"

"Charlie, you heard her last night. She said it was to make an announcement and she said it probably didn't concern anybody but herself but she wanted to make it publicly."

Well, you can't talk and run the way we were running from a dockside warehouse to Moise's place on Bleecker Street and discuss a mystery of this nature in more detail: anyhow, Charlie was half a block ahead of me, a terrific little quarter horse he was with a golden mane. I could hear his boots clattering and once or twice he whooped which I suppose is a Texas cattle-land practice, sometimes he jumps up whooping in his sleep and sometimes with a reason I won't go into.

Moise's front door was slightly open but there was no sign of the lady in the single big room which was her habitation and was at the end of a singularly long narrow corridor (which we called her uterine passage to the world).

We went on in there and observed that she had purchased two half-gallons of Gallo, one white and one red, a loaf of square-sliced bread, a (tiny) bottle of clam dip, a tin of smoked oysters and a tin of sardines.

"I guess it's going to be the destitute lady's shore dinner."

"Let's see what we can do, Charlie."

"Why bother, there aren't even glasses."

"Look!"

I pointed at a fifth of cheap white port which was nearly empty.

"Yeh, I noticed and it was almost full last night so she's already drunk, I reckon."

"But *look!*"

I pointed at a fresh canvas on the easel and it was one

of the loveliest things that La Moise had ever done in her life but it was all in gray and black with hardly perceptible little stains of blue here and there.

"What is it?"

"It's her immortal piece of chiffon," said Charlie lightly.

Being a painter himself, and painters rarely giving each other a quarter of an inch in appreciation, he didn't value the work of Moise as I did. (*A distinguished failed writer at thirty!*)

Then we suddenly noticed that two well-dressed young-middle-aged men had come into the room in silence and were taking photos with primitive box cameras of great simplicity and beauty. The lenses of the cameras were square crystals and the black boxes were so old that they had acquired a purplish patina and glistened in the cold light.

And then the door halfway down the corridor opened and Moise appeared, still clad in the see-through thing she had worn the evening before, hardly definable as a garment, merely a transparency with a narrow opening at one end through which her head protruded and a wider one at the other for her bare feet and slits on either side through which her arms extended at the elbows. Nor did it have, of itself, a definable color other than faint wine stains and fainter dust, with through it the opalescent shimmer of her flesh as she moved into light.

"Moise, shouldn't you be dressed?"

"Yes, completely," she murmured.

"She's in her Halston hostess gown," Charlie snickered. "It's a trend-setter, photographed by Avedon on the lovely Miss Hutton for the cover of next month's *Bazaar*."

She made no response to this except a quick disparaging

glance at Charlie, then turned away from us to whisper something to one of the cameramen.

I decided, however, to be insistent.

"Moise, please slip on something underneath."

"Such as what? Go through my wardrobe, and I'll oblige you gladly if you discover something not contributed to the Army of Salvation."

Charlie turned to me with a grin that suddenly made his face scarcely recognizable to me.

"Hush, let it be," I whispered.

"Please, no whispers around here," said Moise. "Will one of you please shut and bolt the entrance to the tunnel of the unloved and will the others please unfold the chairs and tables for the guests I'm expecting."

Charlie retired to a corner from which he gave me a glance and closed his eyelids on tears. I stood reflecting. Loves come between each other. Although I'd continued to see Moise, since the advent of Charlie, as often as she'd open the door onto Bleecker at her visiting hours, something less definable and revealing than what she wore had descended between us. I think that after Lance's crash through ice, she'd assumed that I would elect no second love but her. But isn't that presuming more than assuming? And my little time of reflection ended where it began, with the one certain fact that loves come between each other: that much was plain and mystifying to me as any rule of nature.

The two cameramen were now photographing Moise as if for some important event in her life, hopping about like slender, elegant frogs, taking their photographs from crouched positions. Her attitude was at once submissive and one that seemed accustomed to provocation. With unexpected ease and freedom, she posed herself for them. It didn't seem at all like her, it seemed like Isadora Duncan posing for Arnold Genthe at the Parthenon somehow.

I swear she seemed like a dancer, and I remembered Lance saying, "Moise is unable to be other than graceful, and I am, too."

(Was this what drew them together?)

•—

I had never seen Moise so beautiful as that evening. Without being conscious of it I moved close to her and closer and then I had an arm about her waist but her face did not alter except that she raised her chin a little higher.

"Moise? Will you please listen to me?"

"No. Will you please shut up?"

"I've got to say something to you before things get out of hand."

"What things do you mean and out of whose hand do you mean? Do you mean out of mine or out of that blubbering fag's?"

"Moise, you know what we mean."

"Yes," she said icily. "Nothing. That's what you mean to everyone but each other, and thank you so much for being so much help with my goddam announcement party."

"Moise, will you clue me in just a little to the nature of this announcement?"

"Eighty-seven years old at Bellevue."

I tried to figure what could be made out of that as a clue-in. It occurred to me that maybe she meant a great-uncle of hers for whom she had considerable attachment since he was her only relative in the world and I thought she probably meant he had passed away at Bellevue, which was plausible enough since he was a charity case in all senses except that he received no charity except a lot of Moise's affection, but somehow this didn't stick as a clue to the nature of her impending announcement. I felt there was danger in pursuing the inquisition but I still was impelled to continue it a bit further.

"Do you mean your great-uncle, Moise?"

"Christ, no. *Patron,* was he a *patron?* How could that old derelict be a patron? A patron is not a parasite, exactly!"

"Oh, *patron,* no, you mean a patron, you've lost a *patron* to Bellevue."

"Christ and his mother, yes, yes, yes, I had a patron till Wednesday night at Bellevue where he expired while handing me nine dollars and sixty-two cents at eighty-seven. Now do you understand or do you expect me to accompany this advance notice of the announcement with finger painting on the ass of that catamite you live with?"

Now these are about as close to her words as I can get now, since I wasn't equipped with a tape recorder that night nor any other.

She was shaking intensely and I was thinking intensely.

Moise had a patron. Well, that figures since she had no means of subsistence that I ever noticed but it doesn't figure that she'd never have mentioned him to me till this moment. But then Moise. How plausible is Moise? I guess about as plausible as her name, as her spectral beauty and as my own definition of myself as a *distinguished* failed writer.

Nothing of much action was yet happening at Moise's, that is, nothing except Moise herself and the slender men in black mohair who were taking pictures of Moise's few finished and many unfinished canvases with their box cameras while the cold light through the windows lasted. Each time a canvas was exposed by Moise to the cameras she would try to shield it from our eyes, particularly Charlie's, but his tears, true or false, were now gone and he merely winked and shrugged at her maneuvers. It was unavoidable that my thoughts should drift back to the lover who had preceded Charlie in my life and the vast difference between Moise's attitude toward him and his toward her from the vibes that existed between her and Charlie. I recalled the night after the loss of Lance, the skater, I had slept with Moise, not sexually but for companionship that night, how neither of us had slept, just lain side by side with locked fingers, and how, at daybreak, she'd turned her head toward me slightly and touched the hair at my temple and whispered, "It is not good but it's God." And I was reminded of a time earlier than that when Lance had spoken of Moise and related matters. He'd said, "Moise will go on for a while just like she is, but, baby, you know and I know that just going on for a while don't make the gig for Moise or no one else. And, baby, you know there's just a few of us and we got to look out for each other."

For emphasis of this wise and important remark, or so it seemed to me then, he clasped my body tight with his long, hard, beautiful legs, then went on to tell me, "My mama in Chicago said to me, 'Lance, God is going to take care of you just like he does of me.' And it was just a month later that I got word from Chicago when I was skating in Seattle that Mama had a big growth in her that couldn't be cut out and that was the way that God took care of Mama and I reckon that's the way he'll look out for us if we don't look out for each other."

I was then young enough to cry very easily without records, and Lance comforted me by thrusting his hot tongue into the ear into which he had whispered huskily those words of dreadful wisdom.

Oh, I know that you know by this time why I am a failed writer and are shocked at my presumption in calling myself a distinguished one, but here an incomplete sentence is coming at you.

They say that O'Neill the playwright referred to it all as Pipe Dreams and sometimes they put him down for it, but if it obsessed him, as apparently it did, I think it was brave of him to repeat it that much: I thought of that because thinking of myself as both failed and distinguished in my vocation is one of those illogical premises to which we must cling for a sufferable lifetime.

Now Moise had turned to me. She was saying, "Someday you are going to wake up, little man, and remember that someone with angelic wisdom once said that ripeness is all."

"Now, Moise, honey, why do you say that to me?"

"Because you are here and you understand English and just don't bug me no more, as Lance would say, about things that concern only me and the possible exception of my last resource in this world, which is Tony Smith in South Orange, New Jersey, and his wife Janie."

Then there was a long stretch of tense silence and to break it I said to her, "Charlie has the flu and the fever makes him silly."

"It must be a constant fever. Let him have it at your place on his own time, and to expose my guests to his flu is a little too much even for the latitude of my tolerance which is wide as the Nebraska plains which I hail from!"

"Now you're beginning to sound more like yourself."

"I don't know what you mean by that remark and I am entirely capable of standing on my feet without your arm about me."

But she didn't move away and I didn't remove my arm.

Her body, thin as a whippet's, was now trembling violently and I did believe that if I released her she would drop to the floor.

No one having closed and bolted the door as Moise had directed, the curious event of the "party" was now under way. Charlie had gone out and returned with paper cups for the Gallo. The first half hour was unnaturally subdued for any kind of social occasion that I had ever attended. It was now dark through the windows and the room lighted only by a thick yellow aromatic candle which had burned down to half an inch from extinction.

I said to Moise, "Honey, that candle is not going to last much longer. Have you got another?"

"No."

"Then let me run over to the Italian Kitchen on the corner and ask them to lend us one."

"No."

"But, Moise, dear, it will be totally dark in here when that candle goes out!"

She trembled even more in the crook of my supporting arm.

"The announcement," she said, "is pertinent to darkness, and anyhow—"

(That is a sentence which Moise did not complete, not an incomplete sentence of my own doing.)

It seemed to me that her voice was as close to expiration as the guttering tallow which filled the large room with a faint, pleasantly sorrowful musk. I think of the word "patchouli" and I throw it in simply because it sounds right.

"Now, Moise, if you are really intending to make an announcement to this strange collection of guests, I think you should do it at once, for when the room is totally dark nobody will know for sure who is speaking even if they can hear you."

"No. Will you please be still. I'm now going to make the announcement."

She did not seem able to lift her voice enough to be heard by anyone much further from her than me in the crowded room, and nevertheless she was making the announcement, and it was obviously intended for everyone present.

"Things have become untenable in my world."

She repeated this statement twice like a judge calling for order in a courtroom. Probably no one heard the statement but me. Her voice was a whisper, and so I took the liberty of repeating it for her at the top of my lungs.

"Moise says that things have become untenable in her world!"

And that was the way the announcement had to proceed. Moise would whisper a sentence and I would shout it. As for the reaction of the guests, or audience, most of them paid no attention but continued their own talk in pairs and groups.

Now Moise was explaining.

"You see, my world is not your world at all. It would be an observation of insufferable banality for me to observe that each of us is the sole occupant of his own world. And so I don't know your world and you don't know my world. Of course it appears to me, it appears quite evident to me, that your world is relatively a world that contains some reason."

At this point she paused for breath and I became aware that Charlie was standing before me with a furious scowl on his face.

"Listen, prick," he shouted, "there isn't a mother in here that's interested in this shit!"

Moise heard him and delivered a slap to the face and a kick to the shin and he moved away, shouting, "Fuck off!"

As he turned in the flickering candlelight, I noticed his ass in profile and exclaimed with astonishment to myself this histrionic thing: "What is life but a memory of asses and cunts you've been into?"

(That isn't at all true, you know, it was just an hysterical expletive of the libido.)

The announcement is continuing as before.

"I think I lived in something more like your world once, I mean a world of reason, but things became more and more untenable and I began to leave the room of that world and to retire into this one. I don't know how long ago."

At this point most of the guests had begun to listen to the announcement but their facial expressions were curious beyond my failing power of description. I can only say there was nothing appropriate in their expressions with the single exception of the expression on the face of an actress named Invicta. Her face was attentive and comprehending: the faces of all the others were—I don't know how to describe it. It was rather like they were in one of those bars in the Village where they show old silent comedies of the Keystone era.

Moise was now mentioning things of a less abstract nature, relevant to her estrangement from the world of reason. She was saying, "My zinc white is exhausted and I have no more blue. I squeezed out my last bit of blue onto my last bit of canvas this last afternoon in my world. Also my black. Gone, too. My cup of turpentine could be mistaken for a cup of gumbo. My linseed oil, gone, gone, and as for my brushes, well, I can paint with my fingers but sometimes I think of my brushes as I remember—*please, are you listening to me?* You look at me so strangely that I can't tell—I think of my dear canvas as of a gentleman who provided me with whatever means I had to continue subsistence. Gone, gone, too, eighty-seven at Bellevue."

She paused, clutching my shoulder in a paroxysm of emotion.

◦

"To have possessed a patron who was a pauper has been the presence of God in my life, but now, oh, now—lived on security, died in charity, where is the poem God now? And the hope of new white, new blue, new black, or one more stretch of canvas?"

I had now stopped repeating her whispers: there was no more breath in me, now, and nothing but, I am ashamed to admit this, but homesickness for the bed in the section of loft and Charlie's fever to warm me.

Much as I do love Moise, when someone you love departs altogether from the world of reason, dubitable as that world may be, you know, you are subject to such distractions from her condition, his condition, whatever, that you

"Moise, please stop now, they're all turning away and the Actress Invicta has collapsed to the floor!"

"What right has she got to give a theatrical performance

during my announcement?" Moise demanded. "Get her up and out of here this instant."

"But, Moise, she is genuinely affected by your announcement, in fact I believe she's the only one here who is at all interested in it besides you and me."

"Hush! The announcement continues!"

And it did continue and I must say that despite the fact that I am accustomed to shocking revelations or confessions, having devoted half my life to them, I was embarrassed, yes, I was truly shocked by what she was now announcing.

"This gentleman, eighty-seven, lost at Bellevue, it is pitiable but not shameful for me to admit this, was, in a sense, my lover as well as my patron. It is probably more accurate to say that I performed for his sake certain little services such as a bit of prostatic massage along with a bit of fellatio and out of his loneliness, the terminal affliction of the old, he would call me his love, and I, well, I was in no position to decline his material assistances, on Saturdays in summer, Wednesdays too in winter, and in spring, yes, actually that season affects the elderly too, more frequent summonses to Apartment F, third floor right, appalling stairs, had to pause for breath on the second landing. And ladies not being allowed there, it was a bachelors' home supported by B'Nai B'Rrith, he had provided me with a tall black hat and a pair of trousers inherited from his father, a rabbi in New Rochelle, to wear when summoned. I received strange glances, caught on the run rushing through, but bus fare there and back was added to the remittance taken out of a padlocked metal box and handed me with whispers of devotion. I don't suppose this belongs in the world of reason. I only meant to tell you that he is gone, too, and I am bereft, I am left without further means to continue beyond this announcement, unless it reaches South Orange. . . ."

She stopped as if to inquire if it would or would not and during this pause in the announcement, which, needless to say, I was no longer repeating, a tall young man appeared directly before us and said, "Unreal, unreal." I recognized this personable new arrival as Big Lot. And then I noticed that Charlie was crossing to him with a cup of Gallo. I caught him by the belt of my army coat which gave him a jolt that caused him to spill the Gallo on my coat and Big Lot.

"Charlie, the party is over,"

"Party, did you say party, and did you mean this one-joint smoke-in without a shot of vodka?"

I looked at Big Lot who said this with one of his impish smirks that enchant some people some of the time and simply seem to be cruelly appropriate to others, the way some people laughed when Candy would not, they say, take the chemotherapy treatment because it would make her hair fall out. But I had stopped interpreting the smiles of a winter night and I only said lamely, "If it wasn't a party, wouldn't you be in the bushes on Central Park West?"

"No, baby, in the trucks with some old trick of yours!"

It was not a scintillating exchange of bitcheries nor was it meant to be, and Big Lot's baby-brown eyes turned upon Charlie with a dreamily appraising up-down look.

"Why don't we go down to Phoebe's for some chow, it's a night for hot chili."

He hardly returned his look to my direction as he ordered me imperiously to give Charlie some cab fare.

"What is a cab?"

"A four-wheeled conveyance used for urban transport by successful writers."

Allusions to my calling always score painfully when made by faded friends and I never answer, but Moise had emerged from her moments of inner reflection. She said to Big Lot, "It's a distinction to be a master of anything, which includes the cunning of betrayal."

Her ice-gray look removed the languidly supercilious smile of Big Lot as if his face had never worn it. Hurt and anger flashed there.

"Oh, for Chrissake, Moise, it's me that betrays himself to everybody, not anybody to me or by me, and whatever this fucking gig is I find it too unreal to believe it and personally not being into the theater of the ridiculous, I'm going to Phoebe's for vodka and hot chili and no shit about betrayals."

"Watch out for the sudden subway," Moise said softly as I've read that the *Titanic* first touched that submarine mountain of ice, so softly the dancers in the great ballroom didn't feel it.

("The sudden subway" was Moise's term for all such disastrous inadvertencies as Big Lot is inclined to provoke, less for himself than others, or it may be the opposite way: in either case, it's a tightrope act to

Yes, that sentence is finished in its fashion.)

-•-

The image of ice recurs and whispers, too, and almost subliminally the wire announcing the death of the skater flashed into my mind, and then the night I slept with Moise for companionship's comfort only, our hands touching until daybreak when she placed her fingertips on my temple and said, "Just say to yourself"

Incomplete, there being nothing I could have said to myself except, "Overdosed on blackbirds, a super high, overdosed on a super high in Montreal, a spectacular leap and was dead still skating. 'Didn't come out of the glide. Wanted it so. Audience didn't know I escorted him off the ice, tall smiling dead living.'"

What on earth did she mean by "wire instructions and love"?

A distinguished failed writer at thirty has suspended the climax as if it were a sentence that he had the audacity not to complete.

The Actress Invicta had risen and put on her heroic black cloak as if an imperative such as "À nous le jouer" swept her away

(Period omitted by intent since she stays on.)

An outraged lady once said to me, "How dare you compare him to?"

Each one has his love and comparisons exist in that fact only.

Now back to

Now at this instant the door down the corridor made a loud banging sound as if Moise's announcement party were being raided by the police, it banged the wall that loud, but it wasn't a police raid but something worse. It was the entrance of a certain distillation of venom in the form of a human (?) female called Miriam Skates. I knew it was she who had entered by that inimitable and indescribable shrillness of voice. I know it is a writer's business to describe whatever he sees, hears, feels or imagines but the circumstances under which I'm now writing this thing have made it impossible for me to arrest its present motion by a description of the voice of Skates when she entered the lightless hall: at best I can only remark that probably nothing like it has been heard outside the spectators' section of the old Roman Colosseum in the pre-Christian era when a fallen gladiator was about to be impaled by the victor's trident.

Moise had not moved but I caught hold of her as if she were running and shouted to her, "Moise, you didn't invite her, surely you didn't invite her?"

"Who, who, not invited?"

"Skates, to the announcement!"

"Oh, has she come, is she present? The light's so dim, I—"

"She has just entered with her little company of attendant bitches and there's a dreadful commotion by the door."

"Oh, just arrived. She must have missed my announcement, I'll have to repeat it to her."

"Don't!" I cried out to Moise but she broke away from my grasp with amazing force and started moving toward Skates as Skates started moving toward her. I'm sure it was by intention that Skates arrived at the threshold of the room at the same moment as Moise, no one between them, close enough to have embraced each other had that been their impulse. There was just enough light still coming from the candle for me to see Moise extending her deli-

cate hand toward Skates as if to offer her a polite welcome, and then this fantasy of a confrontation occurred, and before I tell you about it, let me assure you that I am aware of the regrettable sound association between the name "Skates" and the word "skater." You must believe me though when I tell you that the skater and Skates were two polarities, the skater being love and Skates at the opposite pole. All right. Now this is what was now occurring at Moise's announcement party. Skates threw both her skinny arms high into the flickering penumbra by the threshold, her face contorted with loathing, and began to make this loud hissing sound that continued and continued and continued. I will always hear it. It was worse than the hissing sound of any imaginable reptile since the age when the giant ones ruled the earth.

And yet Moise seemed not to hear it at all.

Eventually it stopped, as all things eventually must, and at the very instant it stopped, the candle went out altogether and it was totally black in the room, it was not just black in the room and the corridor but an intensification of black.

But next, and then?

I did not realize until then how dreadfully people fear dark when it is both total and sudden, even when the light that preceded it came only from a candle that was flickering toward its instant of extinction.

The guests were now all in motion and collision. They were tumbling among and over each other in panic toward the door onto Bleecker, that is, all except Moise and Skates and myself.

Skates struck a match and resumed her hissing. And Moise, still seeming not to hear it nor to have noticed the flight of guests, repeated her announcement with slight variation.

"The world of reason has ceased being tenable to me. It was once somewhat but now is not anymore. I have used all my paints to exhaustion, linseed and turp are all gone, brushes worn to bristles on splintered sticks. So matters stand, you see, and to say that they stand may seem ironical to you, if this were a time when"

"*Sssssssssss!*"

"Since matters in such a state cannot be thought of as standing nor as standable, either. However"

"*Sssssssssss!*"

"However, in all circumstances, before accepting surrender, one last resistance seems required by the nature of all still existent."

How long it might have continued is a matter for speculation had not the little clutch of attendant bitches behind Skates, probably feeling that she had scored her point, begun to draw her back along the corridor to the street, some striking matches as they moved her, and it made me think of how the Queen Ant is moved by the colony and that is an incorrect statement for at that moment it made me think of nothing: it makes me think now, in retrospect, of a malignantly fertile insect, yes, perhaps a sort of huge driver ant being hauled about by drones in the colony of malignant creatures, a thing I once saw magnified by a microscopic lens in a copy of the *National Geographic*.

-

Last month received a rejection slip from a little mag called *It Is* and the Editress had scrawled on the slip, "Incoherency is but is not." Oh, well.

Of coherency, I usually attempt it.

I was now alone with Moise, I mean I was *then* alone with Moise. We were not visible to each other but our hands were in contact.

"Was that Skates at the party? Did she hear the announcement? Was someone blowing a whistle? The light was so dim that—"

"Love, don't you remember?"

"Did they all?"

"What?"

"Go before the request?"

"No, no, if you mean Tony."

"I meant Jane too."

"Of course, and I think the actress"

"But she lost consciousness, she, she *did*, she fell down, I think she meant well but she fell!"

"Moise, dear, things will be repeated, it was that sort of occasion when things will be repeated via the grapevine. Time, it may take time, and Life and Fortune and People, but things will be reported about the party and eventually"

"Yes, I know, I know. And so the party is over."

I think that I was beginning to catch Charlie's fever since I broke into song.

"The party's over, the candle flickered and dimmed."

Not very funny, but then

"Go, dear. I have to pray. I do it better alone."

And so she dismissed me, gently.

All the way back to the rectangle with hooks I sang that song which now makes me cry. Do you remember? *Killing me softly with his song* . . .

I am sure that by this point you have come to realize that present conditions are distinctly unfavorable to putting things in order.

Without expansion of that remark, let me include a slight account of a close call to an encounter between Moise and Skates at an occasion a month or so previous to the announcement party.

It was the exhibition of Don Bachardy's portraits at the museum near what was once called Columbus Circle and maybe still is.

I went with Moise.

We had been there admiring the portraits for less than five minutes when a great commotion occurred near an elevator door which had just opened. I recognized the cause and I turned Moise away from it.

Yes, it was Skates, attended.

She was scarcely out of the elevator, possibly still in it, when that phenomenally shrill voice cried out, "My God, an exhibition of realistic portraits just when my non-portraits are catching on!"

Variations upon this outcry were echoed by her attendants. The effect was rather chilling on the large room although it was crowded to capacity and the body heat was sufficient to have made it comfortable without radi

Sorry. Do radiators exist in the world anymore?

The next thing I knew was that in this chillness a great man of letters—was it Isherwood? Christopher, yes, of course—had gone straight up to Skates as if unaware of danger and had said in a loud, very clear English voice, "Did I hear you say non-portraits?"

"Sssssss!"

(Echoed by attendants.)

"What are non-portraits, if you'll explain the term, are they portraits which are not portraits, and if that is so, what are they?"

"Sssss!"

(Echoed by attendants.)

And on that occasion, too, the attendants removed her from the scene as a massive female insect, dedicated to the reproduction of the species, venomous, is removed by its drones.

◆

I would say it took ten minutes to remove the vapor about the elevator by which Skates had arrived and departed with her attendants.

Moise seemed to be unaware of what had occurred.

It was only on the subway going downtown that she remarked after a long reflective silence between us,

"I suppose."

"What?"

"Skates."

"Yes?"

"Is inclined to"

"What?"

"Realistic self-portraits of a certain nature."

"I know, but being deluded"

"Oh, deluded, no. I think she is quite at home in the world of reason."

I am sure that you must see, now, why I thought it appropriate to squeeze this account of the previous encounter, such as it was or wasn't, into my last Blue Jay notebook.

It's seldom my practice to observe sequence. When I try to, my thoughts blur and my fingers shake but these being the final three pages of my last Blue Jay, I have a sense of time running out on me faster than running in, and it is surely advisable, then, to include at once the reason for the rage of Skates at Moise. I shall tell it badly but I shall tell it as best I can.

About two years ago, the artist-teacher Tony Smith referred favorably in a lecture at Hunter College to the work and character of Moise. The reference was to the effect that the purest painter now painting was a child of God called Moise and that she was enduring an existence impossible to sustain because her primary excellence in her vocation, the purity and austerity of it, made it psychologically impossible for her to exhibit during her lifetime. This reference to Moise and her work was noted by a friendly acquaintance of hers on the staff of *The Village Voice* and it was printed, the reference by Smith, in that gazette. Moise did not refer to this reference, never, but it was the first bit of real encouragement which she had received and it had, I infer from her announcement last night, made of Tony Smith of Hunter College and South Orange, New Jersey, and the world of Western Art, a God to Moise.

I feel a bit of confusion coming on me and if I were on a plane there would surely be an announcement: "Please fasten seat belts, we are about to enter a bit of turbulence."

(I've never been on a plane but "the living nigger on ice" was often on them and he told me of these announcements which always amused him so that he would howl with laughter at them, he told me.)

Now I have got to discontinue this thing for a while, even though I never ignore the possibility that some inadvertence, a sudden subway of sorts, may stop it permanently in its tracks as Mr. Eighty-seven at Bellevue.

Rest, breathe, recover if you can, the cry is still *En avant*.

＊

I suppose it is simply and inescapably human to attribute all defections on the part of your loved one to some influence other than what is the commonest fact, an insufficiency in you to his requirements of a lover. Such an admission is quite inadmissable at first, so you attribute it to some external thing such as fever and the unsettling announcement party at Moise's. This gives you an excuse to make all dignified and many undignified efforts to recover him from the seductor. "Seductor" is not a true word, I'm afraid, but never mind, let it pass. I'm sure you know what it means. Later on you will be obliged to accept that commonest truth of the matter, assuming there's truth in matter, that he has simply latched on to a new and more magnetic attraction than you have presented to him, and that later-on moment is probably the moment when you stop being young, even though it may not whiten your hair at the temples prematurely or score its impact with deeper lines in your face.

I did not feel at all young anymore when I entered Phoebe's and looked all about, including the men's room, and discovered nowhere in that oasis of chic on East Fourth Street a sign of Charlie and Big Lot on their vodka and hot chili date.

After prowling the premises in this houndlike fashion, I inquired of the barman if Big Lot had been there with a long-haired boy.

"Big Who?"

"Lot."

"Never heard of her."

I was only slightly comforted by the fact that the barman at Phoebe's disclaimed any knowledge of Big Lot, whom I'd assumed to be known in all fashionable resorts both uptown and down, and the barman had even referred to him by a female pronoun.

Well, there was no reason on the conscious level to continue along East Fourth, but possibly on the unconscious level, with which I am more familiar, it seemed appropriate to move closer to the Bowery. I was frightened across the street by a very tall, raggedy speed freak leading a reluctant dog past me with a metal chain that was not an ordinary leash but more like those things you see displayed in leather bars for the giving and receiving of correction. The tall frenzied man suddenly snatched the chain off the whining dog and began to lash the poor creature with it, apparently for its failure to keep pace with him. This was just under a streetlamp and I saw that the dog was covered with sores new and old, in fact his long muzzle was hairless and blood-stained.

"Stop it, stop it or I'll report you!" I shouted.

The dog-beater instantly lifted the metal chain, preparing to lash at me with it, but while the chain was still above me I scuttled across the street to an area of brilliant light which was cast upon the pavement and the curb by the lighted marquee of a far off–Broadway theater called the Truck and Warehouse.

In this protectively lighted area I looked across the street and saw that the large cadaverous dog was chained again and trotting desperately alongside his owner-beater, around the next corner where I'd been headed.

In a hazy way I thought, "Well, that's how it seems to be," meaning between two desperate living creatures. I stood there and hazily pondered this subject for a while and then dismissed it as self-pity and negativism since in my heart I knew that two desperate living creatures are more often inclined, if they share a life together, to care for protectively than to abuse each other.

(An often beautiful thing in a frightful world.)

I began to be aware that a public rehearsal or performance was in progress inside the oddly named show-place where, I remembered, an unexplained explosion and fire had terminated the run of a previous attraction.

I was obstructed on the pavement beneath the brilliantly lighted marquee by the figure of a bum sprawled horizontally across the full width of the walk as if he were planted there as a prophecy of doom for the theater's present attraction, but he was not too unconscious to raise his head slightly and ask, "Can you share some shange?"

"Sorry, but not after taxes," which sounds like a cruel response but was intended as humor.

Then there was the crash of a door thrown violently open and a short, stocky little man burst out of the show-place, exclaiming to himself, "Awful, just too awful!"

He was in a fur coat of some kind which made him resemble a stunted bear or an overgrown muskrat.

Both this fur-coated man and the lying-down bum were now on the pavement before me so that I was compelled to hesitate there for a moment, during which the short man continued to cry out to the night air and himself, saying, "I swear it's just too awful to believe."

Then his look encompassed my presence which he admitted by saying directly to me, "Do you know what I mean?"

I said "Yes" without interest but he continued to stand in my way and was now catching hold of my arm:

"I certainly had no desire to take over direction, but I felt obliged to since all the stage movements seemed to be arbitrary. I mean that the actors were crossing back and forth, I suppose with the intent of providing the play with an air of animation, it's a very talky play, and I liked the director but I couldn't accept this manner of trying to animate it, and someone has just told me that when I took over the direction the leading lady said to the stage manager, 'Why should I take direction from this old derelict?' "

He seemed to be an aging man with poor eyesight. He thrust his face forward and changed glasses.

"Haven't I met you somewhere sometime before?"

I returned his closer inspection and said, "Yes, at Moise's several years ago. You seemed to be in a stupor."

"And didn't I?"

"Yes and no. I mean you"

"Tried?"

"You offended my friend by placing your hand on what was his terrain."

"Oh, I"

"I explained to my lover that it was just one of those automatic gestures that come from habit."

His attention blurred and I started to extricate my arm

from his grasp but he tightened it on me and said, "Did you say Moise?"

"Yes, I was there tonight and"

"How's Moise?"

"Are you interested or just asking?"

"Yes."

"I think she's not very well."

"I think I had the same impression of her."

"Oh, were you there?"

"Yes, that's where we met."

"I mean tonight."

"No, I haven't been to Moise's since that Oriental with you said that he would print me on the plaster with a smile."

"He was not Oriental. I think I have to go on now."

(Actually I did feel that I had to go on since this was an encounter that seemed to have no purpose and my head felt like it was suspended yards above me at the end of a string that was about to release it. But the little animal-like man said, "Please walk me to the corner, I can't make it alone.")

We stood on the corner, and now I could see that he wasn't drunk or stoned but very ill.

This observation didn't concern me much but being from the South I felt that I shouldn't ignore it.

"You don't seem to be well."

"Yes, and there aren't any taxis."

"Taxes on what?" I said with a touch of malice.

"Everything in existence. Let's go in that bar on the corner for some wine and if they won't call us a taxi I'll order a limousine from Weber and Green."

"Sounds like a vaudeville team."

"Yes, most things are, and they look like funeral cars."

◆

I took him into the bar on the diagonally opposite corner and the moment he entered he was seized by a crazed sort of exuberance.

"I cry for madder music and more wine!"

The bartender looked at him with disparaging recognition and paid no attention to the outcry, but the little man fell into a chair at a table and began to stomp his feet under it.

A kitchen employee came out with catsup stains all over his apron. His attitude toward my accidental companion was friendlier than the bartender's: at least he said, "Glass or bottle?"

"Bottle and two glasses!"

Then he went over to the box, deposited a quarter and punched one number three times.

Now this is somewhat amazing but it turned out to be the Lady in Satin singing that old favorite of mine "Violets for Your Furs."

He came back to the table and simultaneously two things happened of the automatic nature. He kissed me on the mouth and I started to cry.

The whole evening and night seemed to have been served in a concentrated form, like a bouillon cube dropped into a cup of hot water, on that Bowery table.

The bottle and the two glasses were on the table now and he was touching my face with a paper napkin.

"Baby, I didn't mean to do that, it was just automatic."

44

(He thought I was crying over his Listerine kiss which I'd barely noticed.)

He slumped there drinking the dago red wine as if to extinguish a fire in his belly, the rate at which he poured it down him slowing only when the bottle was half-empty. Then his one good eye focused on me again but the luster was gone from it and its look was inward.

"You have encountered a wino."

"Appropriately in the Bowery."

"After the first glass I can't tell a vintage château wine from this bilge served here or even *rouge* from *blanc*. Did you know that the man who wrote *The Shanghai Gesture* wound up in the Bowery, too? I mean he created the part of Mother Goddam for old Florence Reed and it made the producers a fortune but he died in a Bowery gutter a lot younger than me. And do you know his name?"

"No."

"Well, such is fame, I can't remember it either, just the first name, John. It wasn't a good melodrama but it contained a wonderful speech or two and as a farewell gesture I would like to revive the Florence Reed part in drag.

"In my youth," he continued, "I was so shy it was difficult for me to talk but now I've become a garrulous old man who is full of anecdotes that pour out as the wine pours in."

I replenished my glass while I had a chance to and his one good eye, similar in color to the two eyes of Moise, turned more deeply inward.

"I'm afraid I've lost your attention," he observed sadly.

"I'm afraid you did. I was remembering something."

"I asked if you liked poetry."

"Why did you ask me that?"

"Because you look like you might."

I decided to use diversionary tactics.

"How do people look who like poetry?"

"If they like lyrical poetry, they sometimes have eyes like yours."

"And if they prefer epic or intellectual poetry?"

"Academic, perhaps. You never can tell. Take Wallace Stevens, for instance. He was a great lyric poet and also an executive of an insurance company in Hartford, Connecticut."

I thought perhaps I'd succeeded in my tactics as a blank look had appeared on his face, but then I noticed that he was removing a crumpled piece of paper from an inside pocket.

"Sometimes I do like poetry, some of it sometimes, under some conditions, but not right now. I don't want to read it or hear it read to me right now."

Then I saw that my alarm was unjustified as it was only a piece of Kleenex that he had removed from his pocket and he wiped his watery eyes with it.

"I began with poetry and I think I might go back to it. It's cheaper to produce and I think that the current standards are even lower. Of course all forms of self-expression serve the same purpose."

I didn't ask what purpose but he continued as though I had.

"To get you out of yourself."

Then his look turned inward again: I felt released, not from my self but his. I suppose he was sorting through his sixty-odd years of recollection like a pack of old Tarot cards and, looking at him without much interest during his period of introversion, I wondered about his ethnic origin. If he were a Jew, he must have been a Sephardic one, the kind that never wandered but stayed in Spain. Or have I got that backward? But he did seem more like a creature whose parts derived from foreign places and were only assembled in the States. Perhaps he was a kind of Gypsy, and as if he divined my speculations about him, he leaned back dreamily in his chair and said, "Since I left home in my teens I've always lived a nomadic sort of existence as if I were looking for something of vital importance to me which I had lost somewhere."

"Are you giving an interview to me?" I asked him with a touch of asperity.

"Don't be bitchy, love. You're Southern like me and we have to be gents."

"Not when deserted by the second love of your life, a youth who was designed by Praxiteles."

"An artist of the world's first and last democracy. Was he blond as I've heard the early Greeks were and was his skin?"

"What?"

"Flawless ivory wedding-gown satin smooth?"

"You left out warm."

"Oh, that comes with it, the body provides the warmth."

"Especially with a fever."

"All worthwhile brides, or loves, run a little temperature, baby."

"For a little while. They cool off."

"Even the sun cools off."

"Gradually, not suddenly."

He nodded slightly and his look turned inward again.

"The effort of making a comeback is an inadvisable effort because it exhilarates you at first like a speed shot and then you crash. Sometimes what seems like a trivial thing will do it, like a letter being omitted from your first name on the *Times* drama page. What was, where was? Oh, yes, I love to travel. I had a fellow traveler of my own gender and inclinations till four packs a day and Memorial took him, all but his pride was removed. Stayed till he went away."

"I think I ought to go now."

"Yes, he went. Dignified and lonely as a comet through space."

He smiled as if he'd accomplished the dignified flight with him.

"Shouldn't you call that cab now?"

"Oh, and this evening, or some evening this week, I read about an astral phenomenon called a quasar and learned that it is the nucleus of a new galaxy in the sky in a state of formation through expansion and that it's, I'm no good at fixtures, sorry, I mean figures, but I believe they said it was two million or billion light years away and was the most distinct and so was presumably the closest to you and me sitting here. Sorry. My brain was damaged by three convulsions in one morning at Renard Division of Barnes so there is rarely much comeback to clarity now."

My attention had begun to turn upon him with more interest now, since he'd also suffered confinement, and I noticed that a fleeting illusion of youth had appeared on his face, the lines still quite apparent but a ghost of a much younger face appearing through its descendant.

"We were flying from L.A. to San Francisco on a two-prop plane back somewhere in time and we were over mountains when the stewardess passed down the aisle, she was trying to reassure us about a mechanical failure of the plane. She said loudly in a quavering voice. 'We are turning back to Los Angeles because one prop has failed. Don't be alarmed if we start losing altitude.' Well, I was petrified with alarm despite her injunction against it since I could see out the plane window that we really were dropping toward the mountains and I said to my beautiful young companion, 'I guess this is it.'

" 'Forget it, I've flown over the Pacific, a parachuter in the war, in planes riddled with flak, with one or two motors gone, and I just ignored it.'

"He had a book in his hand, however, and I noticed that while he was pretending to read it, he was flipping the pages over as fast as if he was looking up a name in an address book.

"I had another idea of how to insulate myself against threatening disaster, since in those days I always went out with a pink barbiturate capsule in my coat pocket. Well, everybody was sitting very stiff and still in the plane as it lost altitude but I got up and went to the lavatory and dropped the pill, and when I returned to the seat beside my friend, I was calmer than he was. He was still flipping the pages of the book faster than a human computer could read but I was so tranquilized that I put a hand on his thigh to reassure him as well as to enjoy its familiarly dear contour.

" 'For Chrissake,' he said, 'Don't make a *brutta figura* in front of the stewardess and the passengers on the plane.'

" 'Who's looking at anything but his own terror?'

" 'Look, if we don't take another plane to San Francisco tomorrow you won't have the guts to ever take another flight again.'

"And about noon the next day we did take another plane to Frisco. But it was a four-prop plane. You see, in those days I had someone to control my panic and arrange my life for me, but now I have got to manage it alone except for short-term companions."

He'd ordered another bottle of the dago red since I had finished the second half of the first during his anecdote.

He was well into this second bottle and into his next anecdote.

"I've been solaced till lately by the traveling companionship of a lady I knew who was as restless as I am."

(I wondered why he said *knew* instead of *know,* and *was,* not *is,* but that was to be revealed.)

"One spring we flew from Athens to Rhodes, I mean the Greek island, baby, and a big contingent of the U.S. navy was in the harbor there, too. We were sitting outside a waterfront bar admiring the electric display which the navy boys had rigged up before they came ashore. There was a particular sailor on shore that outshone the electric display and appeared to be in hilariously good and responsive humor, so I turned to this great lady at the table with me and began to complain about our hotel accommodations on the Island of Rhodes. This was a new hotel, set far back from the harbor, and it was a baffling maze of steep ramps and stairways which I found it difficult to steer my lady friend up when we went home after midnight. I said to her, 'Honey, you know we can't stay another night there and you know the only good hotel on this island is the Hotel des Roses straight to the left a little ways down the street. Now why don't you go over there and turn on your Southern charm and book us in there tonight for a two-week stay?'

"This lady-companion, being a really great Southern lady, would never refuse a heartfelt request like that, so off she wobbled down the waterfront to the left toward the

Hotel des Roses, and I was then free to concentrate on the hilarious sailor but it soon turned out that he was more responsive to a navy buddy than he was to me, so I had to sit there downing one ouzo after another for an hour before my lady-companion came wobbling back out of the dimness of the beyond and as she came into the light I noticed that the front of her pink skirt was almost entirely covered with a dark stain and as she came still closer to the waterfront table, I detected an odor of piss.

"I said, 'Honey, it looks like you spilt something liquid on your skirt,' and she lurched into a chair with a raffish grin and said, 'Yes, well, on the road I was forced to urinate and there wasn't a ladies' room visible along there, so I just squatted down in the road and let it go.' "

At this point he leaned back in his chair, laughing, and fell on the floor, but seemed not to notice this incident, just picked the chair up and sat down in it again and continued his story.

"So I said to her, 'Oh,' and then I asked her if she had booked us into the Hotel des Roses.

" 'No, honey, negative there. The desk clerk tells me it's booked up solid as a rock for the next six months or more.'

"Well, I should've dropped the subject but it was so intriguing, I asked her,

" 'Did you, uh, pee on the road before or after you got to the hotel?'

" 'Why, naturally, *before*. You know I've got a weak bladder and I certainly didn't want to commit a public nuisance in the hotel lobby.'

" 'Oh, so, *before*. Well maybe, honey, that had something to do with their being booked solid for so long in advance.'

5 1

"That sounds like a bitchy remark for me to make to this great Southern lady, but it didn't phase her, nothing much phases a lady. She looked at me and grinned. It was a crooked pirate's grin, an oh-fuck-it-all sort of grin which had great charm and distinction, I swear it did. She was what the French call a *jolie laide*, which means—"

"I know French. It means pretty despite."

"That's right, despite everything. God, how I loved that girl."

By now we'd finished the wine and had caught a cab.

My chance companion had sunk into a mood of revery and sorrowful regret.

It didn't particularly concern me but I asked him, out of politeness, if he was still traveling about with this *jolie laide*.

"Grinned like a pirate but was an absolute lady."

"I asked if you still travel with her."

"No, not now, how could I? Smoked continually, fifth of bourbon, quart of Scotch a day, with double martinis at meals, no, I'm not traveling with her, God rest her soul full of love."

"She's, uh, taking a cure?"

"She's taking a rest in her heavenly mansion."

"Oh. Departed."

"Tha's right, too far to follow. Complications of cirrhosis and emphysema removed her from this world and left me stranded."

He changed his glasses and peered at me in the cab.

"You like travel?"

"If you mean would I like to replace her as your traveling companion, no, I wouldn't, no further than West Eleventh."

He'd told me such a sad story that I began to shed tears as if I were listening to Lady Day again.

"Didn't mean to distress you."

As if to console me for a loss as great as his own, he began to stroke me here and there and God knows where it would have been next if the cab hadn't lurched to a contemptuous halt in front of the dockside loft.

I said, "Thanks for the ride," and sprang out.

"Oh, do we get out here?"

"I do but not you."

"Why?"

"Because I live here."

"In a place this big and dark? Nobody could live here!"

"No, but I do."

He gasped and said, "God almighty! I didn't know you were *dead!*"

"Forget it or fuck it."

"Baby, I meant I thought that only *I* was. The single tenant of the great ebony tower! I didn't know that we occupy the same world. *Hey, wait!*"

I don't know if he meant me or the cab, but the cab lurched quickly away, and I am not at all sure that reporting this encounter in such detail is justified by the few little touches of parapsychology in it, faint as the bits of blue in Moise's final (?) painting.

II

WHICH BRINGS ME HOME and alone to my little Blue Jay in the West. I should probably explain that a Blue Jay is a grade-school notebook which is approaching extinction like certain species of real birds. I was so attached to it, the Blue Jay notebook, to the pale blue regularity of its parallel lines on each side of the page, that I had them mailed to me, in lots of a dozen, by their manufacturers in a Southern city that's near my birthplace, Thelma, Alabama. Well, actually, I have them mailed to Moise, since this abandoned warehouse has no mailing address. I can't rid myself of the feeling, even now when I'm thirty, that I am still a fugitive from the truant officer of Thelma. And from my hardshell Baptist mother who hasn't written me, care of Moise, in a couple of years and so may have gone from earthly concerns by this time, including her excessive concern for her only child, which is me. Or have they put her away now, and which would be better? When a person is put away, if it's a woman, she will occupy a rocker in what is called a dayroom. When she is agitated, she will rock fast. When she is sinking into the lethargy of despair, she will rock slower and slower, till finally the rocker stops altogether, and then they are likely to put her on another floor where people exist like vegetables, withering into a equinox which is opposite to vernal.

(Of course I prefer to think that she has departed without stopping the rocker.)

These pencil-scribblings in the Blue Jay, and soon to be on other surfaces available for scribblings, would be illegible to anyone less familiar with my own kind of speed-writing than I am familiar with it to the point of hysteria.

The word "hysteria" derives from the word for womb in one of the ancient tongues, Greek or Latin. I know this because a woman has a complete or partial hysterectomy when all or some of her female organs are surgically removed because of disease or sadistic caprice upon the part of a surgeon.

Deciding to conserve the remainder of the Blue Jay, I start to write upon rejection slips, a great horde of them in and out of their envelopes stashed beneath BON AMI, which is a deterrent to the progress of this thing as I can't help reading the hasty little comments of the editors. The lady editors are consistently gentler than the gentlemen ones who are consistently waspish. One says simply, "Hysterical, see a doctor." Another says, "An inflamed libido, suggest ice packs on head and crotch till corrected."

Yes, I agree, but

I am at home and alone during those wolf's hours that extend in an upward sweep of hysteria from midnight till winter daylight, unrecognizable here since never admitted to the hooked rectangle.

The libido is in the unconscious which is in the thalamus which is in the rear section of the brain which takes me all the way back to my geography classes in Thelma, Alabama, and to the sad but companionable recollection of Miss Florida Dames who taught geography there and who was a spinster withering desperately toward her time of retirement or unmentionable death, which I have just now mentioned as one is compelled in a dream to open a closet door despite or even because of one's intense dread of what it is closed upon.

And back, now, to seventh or eighth grade geography in the class of Miss Florida Dames in Thelma High Junior and Senior. And it is drawing toward spring, the air is infected with a sensual languor, the sort of atmosphere that exists and prevails in my Blue Jays.

(Came very near saying "blue jeans.")

And fatally one day Miss Dames does not enter the classroom alone but accompanied by her little non-singing canary in its delicately shimmering wire cage and it is as if she had brought along with her an image of her implacable retirement soon to contain her but not shimmering and not delicate as wire with swinging perches for a loved companion. Some girls giggle, some boys grin, and she gives them a little bow of her tight-curled head as if to acknowledge a modest round of applause and she then nods encouragingly to the canary and she places the cage on her desk, remarking, "It was so frightened today I couldn't leave it at home," and even the most insensitive clod in the class must have sensed, at least dimly, that she was referring to her own fright more than to the canary's. Then she sits

57

down and says, "If it disturbs anyone, please raise your hand and I'll"

She didn't say what: I don't think she meant she'd remove it. I think that Miss Florida Dames was terrified of being without her canary, yellow as butter in a wire cage yellow as finely spun gold.

However, its presence didn't calm her nerves any more effectively than her nerves calmed the canary. She became more and more agitated as if there were a storm of wings in her narrow chest and her necklace of coral shook and her voice shook with it and the canary hopped about with more and more agitation, in precise correspondence to hers.

"Roger, will you please"

(She stopped, gasping for breath.)

"Pull down the"

(Gasp for breath.)

"Map of the world I received from the P.&O. Lines in Mobile?"

He was a tall boy in the front row and when he rose after long hesitation to comply with her request, the fly of his corduroy pants bulged as if he'd been entertaining libidinous thoughts concerning Miss Dames or her canary or the very large colorful map of the world. She had often informed us it was presented to her by a branch office of the P.&O. Lines twenty-five years ago when she had considered a holiday trip to Hawaii. She had been obliged to abandon that idea for an unexplained reason probably having to do with the expense of it, but she did have the map, courtesy of P.&O. Lines Ltd. . . .

(Limited to what? Her travel expenses that summer? Certainly not to the geographical details of the map.)

Again girls' giggles, boys' grins, and Roger flushing and

shuffling up a narrow corridor of space between embarrassment and pride at the bulge of his sub-equatorial pointer that spring afternoon, and jerking the rolled map down with the violence of a rapist and Miss Dames gasped and her coral necklace bounced on her narrow chest. Girls giggled, boys grinned, the canary hopped wildly about and Miss Dames recovered sufficiently to request,

"Now point out to us the islands called the Marquesas."

(And it occured to me, "Will he open his fly to point them out with his —?")

He stood there, voiceless as the canary and beginning to grin.

"Roger, the *Marquesas, where?*"

The heretofore voiceless canary utters a loud "Cheep" and the classroom explodes with laughter and a moment or two later the door explodes on the principal and he rushes straight up to the desk and grabs the cage handle with one hand and Miss Florida Dames' skinny elbow with the other and shouts "Class dismissed" as he exits with them both from the classroom into the corridor and the uproar of the geography students is abruptly hushed when, at some distance down the corridor, Miss Dames begins to cry out again and again as if mortally assaulted.

I remained after the others tumbled out of the classroom as if it had caught fire, some even out of the open windows, throwing their books before them, but I remained in the warm chalk-smelling room and went up very close to the P.&O. map, looking senselessly for the Marquesas and noticing the Solomons at the top of a long archipelago of little islands called the Louisiade. I see them distinctly now as I did in the desolate languor of that schoolroom in Thelma.

Where is the libido located, inflamed? In the unconscious, of course, as surely as the island of San Cristoval is located at the western end of the archipelago called the Louisiade but much more prominently and in brighter color since it is so inflamed by the absence of faithless Charlie, oh, much more prominently with much more inflammation.

"Hysterical, see a doctor."

Never mind geography and Miss Dames . . .

But I have seen doctors and don't care to see them again, would rather see Big Lot and Charlie intimately sequestered in a dark booth at Phoebe's than a doctor ever again in my life, inflamed libido, hysterical, or whatever.

(I shall have to go on but you may stop when you please. . . .)

And by the way, who are you? I always have to be introduced at least twice as the panic that overtakes me at first meeting a person deafens me to the name.

After a cup of Gallo, "I am sorry, I didn't catch your name," whether or not I wished to, a bit of Southern gentility in my nature or simply

Inflamed libido, liking the contours of . . .

Hawaii 50 is located in the Sandwich Islands somewhere in the suspiciously quivering space between, sorry but never catch names.

But there's one thing about me that you can count on. I am not dishonest. I do not write "unintelligible" or "inaudible" on my transcripts but of course they are nonexistent as the restraints of my libido on the rejection slips of my life or not on old dusty rectangular cardboards that once returned with shirts for love number one from the laundry named Oriental.

I jump up from BON AMI, crying out *Lance* and the outcry

seems to be echoed all through the panicky corridors of my memory, nine-tenths of which are submerged in dark, icy waters like the great iceberg that so gently but fatally nudged the *Titanic* on its first "unsinkable" crossing of the Atlantic, and so I think about death, his completed, mine now surely approaching, and how the band played on in the grand ballroom of that world's greatest steamship, the dancers unaware of what the slight nudge portended.

Lance is reverberated as if through the whole empty warehouse which is the size of my heart at this moment in Blue Jay. . . .

So what do I do? I run to the improvised bathroom and dash the water, miraculously unfrozen, over my face, inflamed as my libido, and I realize that my chronic hysteria is now augmented by Charlie's fever as my libido is by his absence.

What did the ancient mariner say to the wedding guest? Stay with me and I will tell?

A cordial invitation.

A truly confident person is one who does not attend a banquet to which he has been invited and sends no word of regret—compliments of Jules Renard. . . .

Also this: Sarah Bernhardt descends the winding stairs as if she were standing still and the staircase unwinding about her. And in her salon, no chairs, just luxurious furs and pillows on which to recline, and she has five pumas which are ceremonially led in by footmen on chains, yes, both, footmen and pumas are led in on metal chains, captivity, bondage, love.

Success of Rostand's *Cyrano* and her fury that she is not in it for she is not Coquelin, but she carries it off with bravado, she rushes from her theater to his and she exclaims to Rostand, "I hastened through my death scene to catch your last act." And if one artist will do that for another, the world is still not lost.

But that was years later. I also remember this verse about Sarah.

> "How thin was Sarah Bernhardt, Pa,
> That shadow of a shade?"
> "As thin, my son," his Pa replied,
> "As picnic lemonade."

I remember no rhymes about Duse, only that she died in a second-class hotel in an American city of no distinction on farewell tour. But I recall one more about La Bernhardt.

> Sarah Bernhardt had one leg,
> The other was a wooden peg.
> But good she did, yep, she did good,
> Clumping on a stump of wood.

Yes, I am with the clock which locksteps with me martially through the wolf's hours till morning. I say *alone* with the clock and underline alone to mean more intensely alone. Of course in a sense I am also with the Blue Jay, but in a stronger sense the Blue Jay is an extension of myself and so the accurate thing to say is that the Blue Jay and I are alone with the clock.

And the wolf has a varying number of hours, not just one. I would say that the wolf's hours are those spent alone, uncomforted by sleep, during a period of night, post meridial, when you are accustomed to a loved living presence which is not that of a clock, nor even of an "extension of yourself," although

It is now after two by the one-legged clock which I have

placed as far away from me as the limits of the rectangle permit, not only because its noise is much too assertive tonight but because it is the subject of Charlie's latest painting, executed in the style of that progenitor of pop art, Mr. Gerald Murphy. To do this sort of thing, this marvelously precise representation in pigment of such things as matchboxes and cocktail glasses and the interior mechanism of a watch, requires an all but impossible control of a brush as fine as a penpoint or finer, and Charlie's portrait of the exterior face of the one-legged clock shows an appreciation of Murphy's work and the others of that genre but doesn't approach the marvelous precision which was even more precise than the actual object.

I have now placed Charlie's portrait of the clock in the same place as the clock.

⚓

Fuck you, clock, you one-legged nickel-plated little mockery of my heart, and fuck *les points de suspension* too, those triple dots that betray an unwillingness to call it quits or truly completed. The clock completes each sentence with one tick, they're short and decided quite definitely, and going right on till the clock stops mocking your heart only because it's run down.

An admirable pursuit of a single course, no deviation from it, and one I'll attempt to

But it's no fucking use, deviation being the course of my life.

Chronological order means arrangement according to time: that much I will try to accomplish.

To begin it, a simple declarative statement.

I fled from home at fifteen.

There was much about me like the precocious Rimbaud when he started his literary career about five years before its completion. I had the (deceptively) innocent features, the dreamy-pale eyes, the very light and fine hair that stopped the star skater short outside the old San Remo bar, a landmark of the Village (and of my history) which exists no longer. I met them simultaneously, Lance and Moise, they were emerging together from the San Remo, the beautiful light-skinned Negro looming a foot above the crowd at the entrance and a foot above Moise who was exceptionally tall for a lady. They were in the doorway and I was on the edge of the crowd pushing in. I was not pushing in. I am not a pusher of anything but a pencil or pen, and that is part of my huge problem in life. Oh, I know it would have been quite different, my history in Manhattan, if those hazel-speckled green eyes had not slanted down at me from the San Remo doorway with the intensity of headlights turned on me just preceding a crash. The eyes were luminous and they were hypnotic. They blazed at me and transfixed me to the pavement and, well, I wouldn't have moved if I could and couldn't have moved if I would.

I heard him shouting, "Jesus, Moise, dig this dish of chicken *à la reine!*"

(The reference was to me.)

It was Moise who said, "Come along with us, dear."

"I beg your pardon. Where to?"

By this time he had seized my arm as if he thought I could fly.

"Your place or mine?" Moise inquired of Lance.

"Let's introduce him to yours," said Lance. "He don't look ready for the warehouse yet."

"I think I could paint him by candlelight," said Moise.

And so Moise was complicit in my ravishment by the ice skater which occured in her world on Bleecker.

It was a place of curious enchantment from the first. The one great window in the back wall of the room was glazed with frost which refracted the gleam of that almost indispensable accessory to her life, the amber-tinted aromatic candle set upon a blue saucer. And as I went down the long corridor into the room, I felt that it was unheated except by the entrance of Lance. He gave it warmth and vibration which made the frost coating on the window crack a little.

"How nice to get in out of the cold," said Moise. "Please excuse me a moment."

She then retired to her bathroom where she remained long enough to plaster and paint the walls.

"Where you come from, baby?"

"From Alabama."

"Where stars fell one night?"

"Oh, yes, I"

"That's a long haul, you better lie down and rest and recover your breath. You are panting like you'd run the whole way."

"I had no idea the city was so big."

"You ain't seen nothing yet."

＊

When Moise returned to the room the skater's long legs had a scissor hold on my body, there was blood on the bed, the burning eyes had blurred with loving contrition.

Moise was the soul of sympathy and discretion. She made no reference to what she observed or what she had heard. She was almost soundless in her goings about the room, fetching a towel and glasses of red wine.

I recovered enough to say, when she offered me the red wine, "Do you think that'll put a little blood back in me?"

Well, actually, I hadn't bled all that much despite my defloration by the well-endowed light-colored black ice skater.

Now I know I have said that everything in the last fifteen years of my life might have been quite different if I had not had this experience which I have told you with that respect for reserve (?) which is the one thing that I hope may justify my claim to some distinction as a failed writer at thirty.

You may very well be warranted in demanding that I explain how such an apparently fairly commonplace experience could have changed my life since then. All right, I will try to explain. For thirteen years after that there was nothing of much importance in my life besides that ice skater and Moise and this practice of mine of trying to write things out in a long series of Blue Jay notebooks.

I may have been a chicken à la queen when the ice skater first saw me but I was not and never have been intended for the use that he made of me that first night, and as I ran my fingers down his silky thighs, I interrupted his whispers to ask, "Isn't it my turn now?"

"Baby, I never took the sheets in my life."

"Yes, but your life isn't over."

With strength from somewhere beyond me, I had extricated myself from his scissor hold and was moving gradually into the dominant position.

"Moise, this chicken is turning to a rooster. Have you got some lubricant in the room?"

"I think there's a bit of petroleum jelly under the bed," she murmured vaguely. "Now please excuse me again. I want to finish a mural in the bathroom."

Even with the lubricant on, I made him say "*Wow!*"

"Too much?"

"Too soon, take it easier, love, yours wasn't the only cherry."

Then, having been joined in wedlock by mutual penetration (a complete sort of wedlock that's often denied to straights), we went to his pad together. It was colder than Moise's, and far stranger, but again his entrance warmed an unheated space.

━

About the homelife, now, in Thelma, Alabama. You've doubtless surmised that I had a possessively devoted mother and a father that loved her but was brutal to me because, when he stumbled home drunk from the stave mill he worked for and the bar he frequented, he'd often find the bedroom locked against him and would break in the door and find my mother clinging to me on the bed as if I could protect her from his liquored ravishment of her.

One night when I was fifteen he snatched me off the bed and shouted, "Get the fuck out of here and don't come back here ever!" which is just what I did, heading North that night like a bird migrating instinctively that way.

They had no idea at home that I'd thumbed my way to New York till six months later when Lance discovered that I was listed among those listed by the Bureau of Missing Persons on a nationwide scale. Well, the Bureau never tracked me down but a few days later I wrote a letter to Mother, giving her Moise's address for mine, and then began the flow of Mother's letters pleading that I come home, which were delivered to me by Moise. At first she tried to get me back to Thelma with pitifully false enticements, such as "Your father is a changed man, quit drinking, and is anxious as me about you." "Son, you must come home, you must continue your schooling and develop your talent, your English teacher has told me you write the most beautiful themes she's ever read in her thirty years of teaching."

But then the tone of her letters changed into reproaches and into confessions of illness.

I couldn't read them alone, I would read them aloud to Moise and Lance.

"Son, you broke my heart and I can't recover, I have lost twenty pounds since you ran away to that city which I hear is a modern Babylon that will ruin you body and soul. The doctor says that my grief has affected my nerves and my heart and is bringing on female trouble.

"Son, you know you love Thelma and you are the star of my life which has not been easy. I'm selling garden products to send you bus fare back here and you couldn't be so heartless as not to return. But if you don't, I will catch a bus myself and come up there if it kills me. So far I haven't informed the truant officer, but you are a runaway schoolboy and can be arrested up there and brought home willing or not. Now please don't force me to do that but you know that I will if you don't. Meanwhile it is winter and you left in wrong clothes. Tomorrow I'm going to pack your corduroy suit and heavy things in a box and take them to the post office and mail them to you at that address you gave me which I suspect is a false one. Now, son, write me at once, say you're coming back to us, don't break the heart of your mother with time running out so fast. *Do not ignore this letter, I mean every word I say!* Your father sends his love. He comes straight home from the mill, never stops off at the bar, drinks nothing but milk and sweet cider."

I read this letter to Moise and to Lance at Moise's.

Moise said, "Love, I think"

She didn't continue the sentence so I don't know what she thought, but Lance embraced me and said, "Child, think of them as dead without recollection!"

The letters kept coming from Mother but this was the last one I opened and read aloud or alone. I kept them all, though. They are still with me now. They are stacked up in a corner of the rectangle, turning yellow from time and damp, and unopened.

But late in April that year my mother arrived at Moise's. She'd come up on a bus line called the Gray Goose and she collapsed at the door on Bleecker when Moise opened it for her. Moise supported her to the bed and gave her an aspirin and a toddy and then she rushed over to the warehouse and said, "Your mother is here in a dreadful condition, you have got to come with me."

I said, "I can't."

She kept saying, "You've got to, you know you've got to!" And she caught hold of my arm and wouldn't let go of it till I went along with her like a marching convict on his way to death row.

Mother was sitting up on Moise's bed when I got there. She had on her good dress, the one that she wore to the Baptist Church in Thelma, but it was terribly wrinkled from the long bus trip and it was now too big for her. I stood there looking in silence as she cried out to me, attempting to get off the bed and toppling back down and babbling away about the reforms of my father and how I was missed by everybody in Thelma and she removed from her purse two return tickets to it on the Gray Goose bus line.

I crossed to Moise's table and stood there drinking her white port till I was able to look again at the babbling ghost of my mother. When I looked at her I said, "You've took off a lot of weight, Mother."

"Son, you know I have worked myself to the bone with the garden products and selling them to the markets. The whole garden's full of products, tomatoes, pole beans, cabbages, carrots, rutabagas and"

She stopped for a moment to breathe, and I wonder if maybe I might not have gone back with her if she hadn't begun to reproach me when she had caught her breath.

"Your father has quit drinking and you have started. You stood at that table drinking liquor till you could turn to face me, your eyes red with the liquor. Now, son, don't bother to pack, we are leaving this awful place right away for the Gray Goose station."

Then I panicked and I ran to the door and out of it, and to my horror, I was pursued by my mother. I looked back and saw she had outrun Moise and was babbling crazily and staggering this way and that. I turned every corner I came to and still she followed. Then I heard a policeman's whistle and I looked back once more. She had fallen onto the sidewalk and was being arrested as drunk.

Still she shouted, "Catch him, catch him, he is my son, a truant!" not understanding that it was her being caught, not me.

I have heard people say they can't sleep alone and others say they can't eat alone or drink alone or simply not live alone or die alone. I have heard many people say they can't do almost anything alone but I have never heard a writer say that he can't write alone. In fact most writers I've known, despite my instinctive aversion to knowing others engaged in the same kind of existence, preferring to know painters and hustlers and practically anything but lawyers and persons who enforce law and others who have commitments to order, an exciting number of whom have recently been exposed as compulsive violators of the same

I know when a sentence is going on too long for the mental breath of a reader not to mention a writer so let me complete what I had started to say and leave it there and go on. I have never known a writer to say that he can't write alone. Now how is that for a simple declarative sentence?

Nevertheless I have always regarded writing as the loneliest occupation this side of death and yet I have the distinction of being a writer who prefers not to write alone, especially after midnight, and I know that there is a contradiction lurking in that statement but I think it belongs there. I think that many contradictions, whether disguised as paradoxes or not, belong where they are because of the contradictions of that four-letter word to which I prefer the synonym of existence and the contradictions of character and of meaning, the contradictions are practically infinite this side of death and I am also aware that I have made three references to death on a single page or surface for words. I think it must be because I am writing alone after midnight. The tick of a clock is the most uncompanionable noise in existence. I call it noise, not sound. It jars the senses more than a garbage truck at this hour. It is so assertively. And I am aware that that is an adverb without a noun to belong to, there are very few violations of law and order in writing which I commit without knowledge. Moise once said, "You are cunning!" and she didn't mean cute. I think it is probably the only thing she has ever said to me which was not intended to be a comfort to me and yet in a way it provided me with a comforting reassurance since I have long, if not always, understood that cunning belongs to the animal side of a man that helps him survive under circumstances not favorable to his survival.

If you begin to write not alone, as I did with Lance the skater and continued for such a long time to, you are not likely to use a typewriter not only because the clatter of typewriter keys is also a noise, not a sound, worse than garbage trucks past midnight, but because you have discovered the purest delight of living which is companionship while doing that thing which you care about even more than lovemaking. . . .

I am writing alone at one twenty-seven A.M. in this hooked rectangle flimsily sectioned off from the desolation of a disused warehouse. Of course I have written alone but less than comfortably always. I have always preferred the presence of a companion. I think, in a way, that is the excuse for the Blue Jay and that I have now accepted it as the only reward in my case.

But when a piece of writing begins to sound like an

incantation, you turn it gracefully there as a practiced skater turns unless you are Gertrude Stein who has forsaken existence or Alice B. Toklas and I am not her, either, although I do sometimes wear a little mustache and take an interest in cooking, at least enough to know when something is on the back burner, and when there is little to cook.

I have mentioned the time, still passing, and the fact that I'm writing alone this passing moment now being announced by the one-legged clock by the bed. I am drunk. I am stoned. I'm alone. You name it, I am possibly it, and there is another contradiction, for I am not alone, I'm with the clock.

⁂

I had my Blue Jays. Lance had his "blackbirds" and his "white crosses."

An unholy trinity of which was or is the craziest I don't know.

Out of almost nowhere I recall a story that Lance told me about the various aberrations of love which he had speed-skated into during his brief lifetime.

After a performance in Omaha, Nebraska, a very youthful fan burst into the men's dressing room, spotted Lance stripping, and tried to thrust a fifty-dollar bill into his hand as he panted, "I want to buy your jockstrap!"

"Yes, he tried to give me the piece of green decorated with General Grant's likeness, and I would have accepted the flattering offer if a late-middle-aged man that was not his legitimate father hadn't burst in there a couple of beats later and snatched him out of the dressing room and I could hear them fighting like wildcats outside it and in the morning paper I read that a seventeen-year-old youth had jumped out of the tenth floor window of a rich industrialist's bedroom. This was the beginning of a two-week gig and a couple of days later the paper said that the kid was going to be buried at a certain cemetery the next afternoon, and I went there with flowers to put on the grave, and I want you to know that a week later than that, the paper announced that the rich industrialist had jumped off the roof of some fat-cat asylum and the paper named the same cemetery where the remains were going to be planted a couple of days later. Well, I thought about you and us and love good and bad and got on a crazy high and did a disgusting thing. I went to the burial service with a spiritual look on my face like I was truly bereaved and I listened to the preacher extolling the beautiful quality of the departed spirit and each time he invented some beautiful quality to extol I made a loud sobbing noise. I had pushed up close to the relatives of the departed who looked uncomfortably cold in their fur coats and anxious to get home. It had started snowing on the casket covered with hothouse flowers and his nearest and dearest were much more interested in the limousines than the eulogy for the departed. They looked like they'd never heard of him except as the President of the Miracle Fiber Plant but I went SOB, SOB, SOB and GULP, GULP, GULP like the printed expressions of grief in a comic strip and all the while I was holding my jockstrap in my overcoat pocket and pushing up closer to the casket with the blanket of roses in the snow, Jesus, I swear this was the scene, out of sight, even the mother of the son of a bitch, she was so old there was scarcely any point in her leaving the cemetery but she was struggling to get on her feet and back into a heated limousine. Nobody seemed to notice her efforts to get up. This was an acid trip I was on, it was after my last matinée in that frozen city and my jockstrap in my pocket was still warm from a performance in it, and do you know I helped the old lady to her feet and I led her to the casket about to be lowered and right in front of her open-mouth face I took out the jockstrap and raised it over the casket and over my head so everybody could see it and recognize what it was and the preacher's and the morticians' mouths dropped open like the old lady's as I dangled it in the snow above the rose-covered casket as it started to be cranked down and I shouted, "This is in memory of the boy John Summers that the departed seduced into death last week in his tenth-floor bedroom," and then I dropped it onto the descending rose-covered casket and hustled the Fiber King's mother to a big black shiny cockroach limousine and pushed her ass in and then raced out of the graveyard like I was high on skates with acid, and, Jesus, yes, did I ever steal that show from the Fiber King's interment, well, I have stopped some shows and I have stolen some shows but never better than that one, and now I know why I did it, it was done more as an expression of social indignation and racial protest than in memory of John Summers or in comment on the Fiber King's black-hearted love and"

He was about to go on when Moise put a quiet stop to it.

"Now, Lance, you know that eulogies are not delivered in graveyards."

75

"No, they're not," I agreed. "The eulogies are delivered in a church and in the graveyard a few words are read from the Book of Common Prayer, so obviously your brain was confused with acid."

"Be that as it may," said Lance, "I had the honor and satisfaction of burying my jockstrap with a king, that I know, and what's it matter if I heard the eulogy at the church or the cemetery, I got a free ride there in a Cadillac but had to go back to the hotel on wings of acid."

"Let's drop the subject," I suggested to Lance since it appeared to me that it was too heavy to hold even with six warm hands in a winter room.

"All right, love, but just remember that I can be meaner than a junkyard dog when the spirit moves me, that's a good thing to know about the living nigger on ice."

Moise drew a breath as long as she was when standing over us seated and touched my head with her hand.

"Take him home for hot chocolate," she suggested to me, and then Lance wrenched me off the narrow bed of Moise with such violence that my shoulder muscle ached the rest of the night and he shouted, "He gets it lighter than chocolate, honey, but it sure is hotter."

On the way back to the rectangle with hooks I began to cry as if I were listening to Lady Day singing "Violets for Your Furs," this being actually the first time I understood about the bad side of love.

It is now ten past four A.M. and I still remain here alone except for Blue Jay and pencil. . . .

—

But I am talking rapidly now, yes, talking out loud to myself as if in delirium which is a practice I have when

I am alone with a pencil and Blue Jay and once it got me into very serious trouble. I was about Charlie's age, passing a glorious autumn in the hooked rectangle, corners softened by the presence of Lance and many things suspended from the hooks, mostly the funky and brilliant costumes of Lance all of whose garments were like professional costumes and nearly all conceived and put together by him who could put together almost anything but his head.

I was not unprepared for the tour of the show on ice but had rejected the contemplation of it as one does approaching death. Still it was coming and one night it came, just after he had come in me.

He said to me, "Well, love, you know the show's going out tomorrow."

"I knew it would be soon but why did you wait till tonight to tell me you're going tomorrow?"

"Why should I let you think about it beforehand and depress us both?"

"I don't think you let yourself get depressed."

"Why should I and why should you?"

"Do you think I'm exhilarated staying on alone here in this corner of a warehouse by the docks while you are performing fantastic leaps and whirls and arabesques on skates in ice-domes over the continent, and no letters from you, just crazy wires now and then?"

"All right. Go stay with Moise."

"That's the least possible thing I could do. Moise is a solitaire when you're not here and so am I and putting a couple of solitaires together does not make a pair."

"Sugar, you and Moise are a natural pair, I always knew you would wind up together when I go through the ice."

"I'm not going to Moise's."

"Then where do you plan to go?"

"I'll take a room at the McBurney if you will pay in advance."

"Honey, if you checked into a Y, you would check out with a board nailed over your ass."

"Are you telling me it's Moise's or else?"

"I think you're wrong about the pairing of solitaires like you and Moise, but"

He got out of bed to pee and when he came back he said, "I will git you a room at the Hotel Earle and pay in advance till Christmas when the show's booked into Madison Garden.

＊

It was there at the Hotel Earle that I began to talk out loud as I wrote and after one week of this, the other tenants, who were mostly retired actresses mainly engaged in comparing their scrapbooks, complained that an insane boy had invaded their sanctuary, that he was babbling out loud all night so they looked like wrecks when they made their rounds of agents and producers in the morning and were being offered character parts for the first time in their lives. Only one of them defended me from the others. She was an actress named Clare something who had made a hit in a play by Steinbeck once. She was a warm and strong-hearted lady but her defense was of no avail since her shapely figure and her superior scrapbook had alienated her from the other actresses there. And so I was hauled off for observation at Governors Island which is a sanitarium in the East River, in case you don't know, and the observation which was made of me there did not result in an early release despite the protests of Moise and Clare who visited me every Sunday. I wasn't working out loud, or working at all, I was mostly desperately waiting for something which was, in my case, the return of the living nigger on ice for his holiday gig at the Garden.

Terrifying experiences like that have a maturing effect, especially in the bin, for even when you are staring vacantly while waiting, you notice certain occurrences outside the storm in your head. I will describe only one. Among the inmates in my ward on the island was a travesty of an aging queen who had entered as a dyed blond but whose hair had now turned silver and who was always in motion, undulating up and down the corridor and around the dayroom, always with a comb in his hand, touching up his curls, and making the mistake of pausing to roll his eyes directly in front of an Irish truck driver who was in there for observation because of nightly wife-beating, whose fists always doubled up tight as evening approached as if he were expecting his wife to appear. Well, one evening this fantastic queen paused in front of him once too often and the truck driver sprang up and smashed a fist in the mouth of the queen, removing all his front teeth. This in itself was not particularly remarkable, I suppose, but what does strike me as deserving of notation as I sit here now with the noisy clock pushing five and still no Charlie, is that the following morning the silver queen undulated again down the corridor into the dayroom, running the comb through the curls with his swollen lips ajar on the crimson cavern of his mouth's interior where those sudden extractions had been performed. The truck driver was seated exactly where he had been the evening before and the silver queen with the crimson cavern stopped again exactly in front of him with the same ocular rotation and the falsetto simper and something happened but I don't know what. I honestly don't remember although I know that something of a shocking nature did happen.

Of course I also know that I have recorded this queen and truck driver scene as if it were comic-strip humor which is certainly not how it struck me when I was twenty.

"Terrifying experiences," "maturing effect," crock of shit . . .

Oh, Christ, now I remember. The truck driver sprang up again and took the queen in his arms and thrust his tongue into the bloody cavern of his mouth with a moan of longing for which transcendent is not too romantic a term.

And so perhaps "maturing effect" is applicable to these experiences after all, despite the fact that I don't know how they matured me nor to what purpose.

••

Just a minute ago I wandered outside of the hooked rectangle we live in to look through the windows of the unpeopled vastness in which the rectangle crouches. I don't remember having ever done that before at night. Well, it is no longer night but after five in the morning which also qualifies as a wolf's hour when it is dark.

My first impression of the dark vastness was one of silence. Then I began to notice little sounds in it, the distance-muted patter of rodents' feet and then the despairing squeal of a small creature assaulted by a larger.

I wondered a number of things: would there be rats in the place if a section of it were not inhabited by human life? I thought, Probably yes, since rats are beings which survive through concealment, in over- and underground places which offer a secret existence from all but themselves and the menace of cats which is to them what Moise means by "the sudden subway" for people. I have a repugnance for rats and all other vermin, although I admire their cunning and their persistence under all circumstances through all seasons. I think they compete with insects and with germs for the honor of outliving man on this earth. I thought of germs, the venereal species, because I was twice infected with gonococci by Lance and also with pubic lice. Having to take a prick and rectal smear test at a free clinic twice was about as humiliating and wretched an experience for me as my stay on Governor's Island, and as for the pubic lice, I have never felt so loathsome. I had never heard they existed until I had them and Lance explained what they were. He was contrite about it but he defended his need of sex on the road with the ice show.

"Baby, if you'd learn to skate I'd get you in the show with me and be a totally faithful lover, but since you claim your ankles are too weak for skating and I am an oversexed cat, once in a while I am bound to infect you with pubic lice and the clap. You know I don't on purpose, it's just that I'm overly sexed and nowadays when I'm high on the streets at midnight and am approached by a good-looking long-haired boy, it's like a call of nature which nobody with an intestinal or urinal tract can ignore."

"Lance, you're rationalizing the negligence of your nature."

"Baby, you know they come at me like flies, I'm not lying, they do."

"Well, why don't you get you a can of fly-spray to carry

in your pocket on the streets after midnight or fantasize your libido like I have to do when you are out on tour?"

"What do you mean by fantasizing your libido, baby? You mean you?"

"I mean I think about you and caress my body at night, sometimes burning a candle and looking at your picture in your tights."

"Do you masturbate, then?"

"No, I don't. It desensitizes your sex and is a messy habit, I just fantasize your caresses over me lightly till I fall asleep."

He held me close in the lock of his legs for a while, then he said to me, "Sometimes I feel like God has given you to me."

He had me stand up, then, and removed from his luggage a bottle called "A-200" containing a pale green liquid which he slowly and thoroughly rubbed into my pubic hairs, around the genitalia, into the armpits, and even over the light down surrounding my nipples. Since the crabs had been burning, it felt deliciously cool and soothing. Apparently it destroyed the vermin at once as well as nearly making me come from his fingers' manipulation.

"Okay, now do it to me."

I gave him the same slow and thorough massage with the excitingly cool liquid, A-200, and this time, rubbing his balls which must have been large as a mule's, I suddenly gasped to him, "Love, I'm about to come."

"Hell, quick, put it in me!"

·•·

Sometimes it's hard to distinguish between a truthful report on your love life and what they call prurience but I don't let it stop me now in these last remaining pages of the Blue Jay which may well be my last ones of all.

I was telling you how I wandered into the area beyond the hooked rectangle of love. It is called deviant love so it's appropriate to "their" definition of it that from time to time one should wander out of its confines, especially when those confines contain no window and you are in them alone and want to see if there is a sign of daybreak.

It was foolish of me to have thought that there would be a sign of it while still in the wolf's hours of winter.

I stood there for a while, my presence known to the rats and making them freeze in motion as addicts of hard-core drugs are said to freeze in motion at times when they feel a strong hit.

Then I turned on my heels and slipped back through a crevice of the plywood that sectioned off the hooked rectangle from the inhuman vastness outside it in the ware-house, wondering once more why it was not condemned and demolished, being so long unused except as a habitation by myself and two lovers.

I smiled wryly and said, "God has forbidden them to"

Then I sat down and said, "It's a monument to the living nigger on ice."

Then, like the cock crowing thrice, I said to myself the last line of a lyric which I'd read once.

"Boys are fox-teeth in the heart."

I recalled that the poem also dealt with girls and with men but couldn't remember what it had to say of them except that it was more flattering and less feeling.

But the feeling was pain and the pain was excruciating and for the third time in my life I seriously considered doing away with myself and by what means I could do it.

(Other two times? When committed to that island in the East River and the first time that Lance infected me with that yellow drip of a pickup on a faraway street.)

Doing away with myself.

On the island in the River East I had thought of slashing my wrists but there was nothing that I could slash them with since they had confiscated my reading glasses, my wristwatch, anything that had glass or a cutting edge to it, except my longing for Lance which was strong enough to draw blood but was not a material thing.

The time of the drip I had considered water, probably because it suggested that old Baptist hymn called "Washed in the Blood of the Lamb."

(Mother used to sing it so passionately in church that people would turn to look at her with startled eyes.)

This brought to mind another short lyric poem on the subject of boys, again just a single line of it.

They offer you their eyes like startled flowers.

(Referring to boys on street corners.)

And I remember saying to the poet, "I think they offer their eyes like broken crutches."

And he replied, "That is because you are negative by nature."

Was that true about me? I honestly don't think so. Not even now as I stare at the next page of the Blue Jay with its pale blue parallel lines still undefiled by the pencil. I don't think it's pessimistic to look upon ugliness as well as beauty bare, although, like Millay and Euclid, I prefer to opt for the second.

And now that next page of the Blue Jay has been fucked by the pencil and is no longer bare beauty. . . .

I am not the only writer in the direct line of the maternal side of my family. My grandmother Ursula Phillips was the widow of a very handsome and dandified young gentleman who was struck by the sudden subway at the age of twenty-seven. By contemporary standards of this Eastern metropolis I don't suppose his accomplishments in the field of literature were particularly striking except in a ludicrous way. His career could be called meteoric. He flashed into it at the age of twenty-two and dropped dead five years later, a burnt-out wreck of a handsome young man who had physical attributes, according to Grandmother Ursula, which would rival Apollo's: a strong but slender physique, flawless skin, large eyes between green and blue which were heavily lashed. "Some people accused him of wearing cosmetics," she told me, "but you know, dear, all that he ever put on was a light cologne called *Lilac Vegetal.*"

When Grandmother Ursula said that to me, I laughed and said, "Grand, do you mean he went out naked except for the light cologne?"

She boxed my ears and said, "Boy, your grandfather was out of blue-grass Kentucky land with blood as blue as the grass. You just remember that and don't make sarcastic remarks which you mistake for humor."

"Oh, now, Grand, don't we all, and nobody means much by it."

"Your grandfather would have spit on Alabama if he'd been the kind that spits."

She creaked up out of her rocker with the intense concentration of those possessed by an idol and brought forth

85

two of her long-lost idol's literary creations. One was a very thin published book, a novella it could be called, which was titled *Edith of*—oh, I forget of what—and the other was a screenplay which he had written when he was picked up by Hollywood as the result of the novella's rather startling success.

"Look here, boy, I understand that you fancy yourself as a prospective writer. Just open this book and read the first sentence of it."

And despite my failure to recall, at this moment, the title of the novella, that first sentence of it is clear in my recollection.

"Edith was a sub-deb, meaning a debutante to be, and it was already apparent that she would be the glamour girl of next year."

"Yes, lovely," I remarked and handed it back to Grand, and then I picked up the screenplay that he had been hired to write on the strength of the book about Edith. The screenplay was of more interest to me then. I recall that I was mystified by the camera directions and the knowledgeability with which Grandmother Ursula interpreted them to me. Of course I can't reproduce the dialogue nor Grandma's technical interpretations at this distance in time, I can only improvise something of a likeness. The setting is/was an exotically furnished pied-à-terre on Sunset, and my grandfather, who describes himself with narcissan extravagance as silhouetted in a damply clinging silk robe against a picture window that seemed intended to present him to public view, much as a master portrait is framed and lighted in a way that is both delicate and dramatic, addresses his lady-companion—presumably my grandmother—without turning to face her. He says to her something like this:

"You know I had no intention of prostituting myself when I permitted my publishers to reproduce on the dust-jacket of my novella a photograph of myself in bathing trunks that were a bit too revealing."

"I don't quite know what you mean," says the lady-companion, obtusely. "I thought the photo was lovely."

"So lovely that it inspired a pederastic producer to engage me to write a film play for a silent-screen star attempting to make a comeback in the talkies."

I kept running into a camera direction called POV, I remember, and Grandma explained to me that it meant the position of the camera, and it struck me, young as I was, that the POV seemed to be rather heavily in my grandfather's favor. Even when the dialogue switched to the lady-companion, who kept expressing remarkable surprise and stupefaction over the fairly obvious revelations which Grandfather Krenning was delivering to her, the POV remained upon Krenning, and I remember that his eyes or his face or his whole being was repeatedly described as "ineluctably" something. Although I had an extensive vocabulary for an early adolescent in a small Alabama town, I did not understand the word "ineluctably." I asked Grandma what it meant.

She replied evasively. "Son, your grandfather was a literary giant." Did she mean that Krenning was a literary giant each time he was "ineluctably" something? I am now aware that to be ineluctably something is to be inescapably something and so it appears to me, now, that Grandfather Krenning Phillips could not have been so inescapably or ineluctably a giant of literature, or prodigal of purity, yes, I believe it was pure that he "ineluctably" was in his own opinion, as the film script indicated.

Well, he kept at it in this scene of the movie. In the idiom of today, he was laying a heavy number on his lady-companion's head with these searing confessions and with his climactic outcry, "For God's sake and mine, don't let this monster corrupt me!"

This cry of appeal left the lady-companion speechless, but the POV remained upon Krenning, in the silk robe that was transparently green as his eyes. Even then I knew there was something wrong there. If the clinging robe was both transparent and green, would it not imply that his skin was also green?

I decided not to ask Grandmother Ursula about the color of her long-gone husband's skin, I let it slide, that question, and simply said to her, "Wow, this is dynamite, Grandma. Did they make the picture?"

"Boy, they'd have made that picture over the dead bodies of the Breen office and the producer whose perversity was exposed in it. So just remember, if you do make it as a writer, and are offered a Hollywood job, turn it down, ignore it, it killed your Grandfather Krenning whom you resemble in everything but height, you're about five inches short of his divine six feet."

"But, Grandma, if he fled from Hollywood to Egypt, Kentucky, why do you say it was Hollywood that killed him?"

"Well, boy, this celebrity thing and this glamour thing which Hollywood glorifies like the golden calf of the Bible, as if without them there'd be no point in existence, is a very hard thing to shake. Now this screenplay for a picture was never shot but a month or two after we were back in Kentucky the very same producer who had seduced my husband sent him a wire: 'Come back at once to star in *Heart Like a Black Jack* opposite the First Lady of the Screen, who is, needless to say, Bette Davis.' This picture was never shot either, but for five years we shuttled back and forth between Egypt, Kentucky, and Hollywood, California, like a couple of migratory birds or more like lemmings, those creatures that swim out from the shore and drown from exhaustion somewhere. I wanted no part of it but the wires kept coming with promises never kept."

"How did Grandfather die?"

"Boy, you have inherited the Phillips talent but also the cardiac weakness which ran in the line. Don't run. Walk. And look where you are going. Your grandfather was enticed back to that city of false hopes and footprints in wet cement and luau banquets by shimmering night swimming pools. Yes, I said swimming pools with blue underwater lights and replicas of coral and of the grotto in Capri, Krenning wrote me and told me about these things with ominous emphasis on the swimming pool and the grotto, the replica of it, and he also told me that the producer would devote a few minutes between tequilas to look over Krenning's synopses and notes and scenarios, murmuring, 'Perfect, a dream, a vehicle for Gary and Marlene! And now, dear boy, how about a dip in the pool to clear our heads for discussion? Never mind trunks, the pool is private tonight, it's just you and me, Ganymede.' Well, Krenning was not a good swimmer, preferred to float alone on a raft of inflated rubber, and had a claustrophobic horror of the replica of the Blue Grotto, but after many excuses not to, he dove in one night and the lecherously enamored producer got him into the grotto from which his perfect young body was removed without life or lights. Oh, my God, I had told him, when you are pursued with lecherous intent by this Hollywood mogul, turn about and kick him in the groin, and maybe he did that when the producer propelled him into the replica of the Blue Grotto, but a kick under water is not effective, you know, it's not an effective kick since it's reduced in speed and impact by the weight of the deep water. Well, at the inquest it was discovered that both of them had on oxygen masks when they dove into the grotto but that one of the masks provided little oxygen while the other provided a great deal of it and I leave you to imagine which was Krenning's and which his seducer's, and at the inquest sexual molestation of Krenning was hinted at but hushed up. Money dies, I mean buys, especially when accompanied by influence of power and position. Of course beauty dies, too, and youth dies, being rarely accompanied by sufficient influence and power, but, boy, remember my advice to your grandfather: whenever pursued with lecherous intent, turn about quick and kick in the—"

"Mother!" cried out my mother.

She had been standing behind my Grandmother Ursula's back for a minute or two and neither of us had noticed her standing there.

"Mother, go to bed, Mother!"

I stood up as the slow procession of the two ladies from my Grandmother Ursula's chair to her tiny bedroom progressed, but just before it was finished, I said to Grandmother, "Don't worry, I'll never go there."

"No, no, no," said Grandmother, disappearing. . . .

❧

I come from a line of disappearing ladies. Once I said to Moise, "I feel that I have a female incubus in me."

She looked at me reflectively for a moment and then said, "There is the *animus* and the *anima* in us all, it's universal, so don't put it down as an incubus which is an evil thing."

"What shall I do with it, then?"

"Use it, baby. What else?"

❧

I am no longer writing in my Blue Jay but on the backs of an impressive collection of rejection slips and the envelopes which conveyed them—I wonder if this is significant? I have a feeling that I am writing in order to avoid thinking of time and Charlie, he ten years ahead of it and I ten behind, and once again the specter of self-pity is lurking closer than the clock in the corner of the hooked rectangle.

But when I say specter I mean exactly that. It is not pity of self but mockery of self and rage at

I've just picked up a particularly depressing rejection slip, I've picked it up because it came in a legal-size envelope with some good writing surface on it. The message of the rejection depresses me to such a point that I feel transfigured by it. I know that this is a peculiar statement. You will naturally think I'm a nut to associate profound depression with a state of transfiguration, that is, if you are not acquainted with a piece of music by the Strauss that didn't write waltzes. He wrote a composition called *Death and Transfiguration.* Of course death is different from depression but they belong within the same general area of human experience, I would say tonight, with Charlie's flu without Charlie.

The rejection slip says to me, "Unsolicited manuscripts are not accepted by *Broom.*" That much is in print on the slip, but beneath this is a furious put-down in red ink by felt-tip pen. It says, "You could be prosecuted for using the postal service for the transfer of such filth. It is not only filthy with prurience but it reeks of self-pity and should be transferred only by a garbage disposal. Sincerely, Manley Hodgkins IV."

It seems to me that I have heard of something called Hodgkins disease and that it affects the lymph glands in a gradually fatal way, so that this editor's name could be interpreted freely as a lymphatic malignancy in the fourth degree which I should think would be fairly terminal.

But what I want to write on the envelope is about self-pity as an element of humanity and of human expression. I think maybe I will merely write out as best I remember a conversation between myself and Lance.

"Baby, you pity yourself and so do I for good reason."

I didn't contest the point.

"But pitying yourself is a top-secret thing that belongs in the little bank vault of your heart until you know how to"

He stopped talking at "how to," but I think he meant how to transfigure it into

You see, I'm not sure, either.

Poetry of humor? Very hard to accomplish, expecially as a skater in palaces of ice nationwide. And yet I once saw him whirl in air with a dazzling smile on his face which contained euphoria along with a sense of doom's approach.

It all ties together except that Lance and not I achieved the approach of doom without a glum expression on the face.

Lance was asleep when he failed to complete his sentence, and I, with my customary sense of the marvelous, very gently picked up the thick and velvety length of human asparagus that sprouted from his bush, half hoping that it would stiffen into erection, and, since it did not, even when tongue tipped, I turned him half-over slowly and entered the velvet of his natal cleave.

To Manley Hodgkins the Fourth this might reek of prurience but surely not of self-pity, which I admit I've never learned to transfigure past depression to a radiant smile in the air.

In Thelma, Alabama, we had warm water that ran all night and I would sometimes slip into the bathroom and run it and soap my prick and thrust it rhythmically between the palms of my hands clasped about it until I came, thighs clenching a corner of the washbowl.

A lonely, nocturnal habit, delicious ejection of the come of creation down a washbowl drain and where it belonged in my instance, which is an instance not suited for descendants.

·◆·

During my confinement to the violent ward on that little island in the River East, I was interviewed once a week by a student psychiatrist whose visits I valued nearly as much as those of Moise. He wore starched white, of course, and was by far the most agreeable staff member to look at. On the days of his visits I would not only bathe with unusual attention to detail but would shampoo my hair with that thinned bar of laundry soap in the men's shower so that my resemblance to the young Rimbaud would be accentuated.

At our last interview he said to me, "I would know without reference to your file that you are a sexual deviant by the way that your eyes drop continually from mine to a part of my body which is only concerned with my wife."

(He may have put it more bluntly.)

"Now tell me," he went on, "have you never had normal experiences of love, in your life?"

(He probably used the word sexual experiences.)

"Yes, once, as a child of thirteen."

He yawned and made a notation in his flipbook as quickly as a mark.

"I see, tell me about it, whom was it with and what was your reaction?"

"It happened in the attic of a little girl playmate. We used to spend afternoons up there in the attic of her home drawing pictures and inventing stories to go with them and once it was very warm, it was summer in Thelma, Alabama, and I noticed that she kept lifting her skirt, which was knee-length, inch by inch higher and separating her legs and finally the skirt exposed her very, very transparent little panties of nylon, light blue, and through them I saw what looked like an indented triangle of a roll, curving outward a bit."

"It looked like a Parker House roll?" inquired the young student doctor with his first show of interest in our talks together.

"What's a Parker House roll?"

"A roll of bread which originated in a Chicago hotel

called the Parker House," he answered impatiently, "and was soon taken up by bakeries all over the country. It was curved and indented at the center and was served lightly crisped and warm. Now continue about this. You saw her pubic area. Was it hairless, still, at the age of, what was her age?"

"Same as mine."

"Now or then?"

(His pace as well as interest was quickened.)

"Then. Thirteen, like me."

"And this inch by inch exposure of her female organ, was it, did you feel it was intended to excite and seduce you or just an innocent way of cooling herself off in the hot Alabama attic, which, what, innocent or seductive and your reaction and hers?"

"Hers was first."

"How, what, go on."

"Yes, she went on with it."

"The exposure?"

"Yes."

"By?"

"Slipping down the pale blue nylon panties inch by inch, too, till they were at her ankles and then lifting her feet out of them and kicking them lightly aside and spreading her—what? Parker House roll? Wider?"

"Oh, then a deliberate act of seduction."

"I, uh, yes, I suppose so."

"Were you, then, capable of erection?"

"Yes."

"And were moved to erection in the steaming attic?"

"Yes, and"

"What?"

"I"

"Look, you're tongue-tied and blushing for no reason, this is a purely clinical discussion. Get right down to the bare facts of it."

"I did."

"Did what did you do?"

"Got down."

"On what?"

"Knees between her knees."

"And, and?"

"Licked."

"Her?"

"Parker House roll."

"Performed cunnilingus on this thirteen-year-old child, you little pervert?"

"Wouldn't you?"

"Christ. Can't you get it through your skull that you are the subject of the discussion?"

"Then why are you erected?"

He covered it with his flipbook.

"Go on, continue, what next?"

"She said, 'Go on,' too, same as you."

"And you went on?"

"Yes, as requested."

"Did you insert your tongue between the lips of the vulva?"

"Yes."

"And then did you?"

"What?"

"Contact her clitoris with the tip of your tongue?"

"What is that word you?"

"Clitoris is the female counterpart of penis except that

it is inside, not out, and is what triggers her climax in copulation."

"Oh, was *that* what it was?"

"Was *what* what it was?"

"A hot, liquid thing happened inside her Parker House roll and she grabbed the back of my head and hollered, 'Can't you lick in deeper?' She seemed to be out of her head and I didn't like the taste of it or my head being grabbed, I've never liked head-grabbing except by"

"Your living nigger on ice?"

"Yes, by him, when he prefers to be sucked than to fuck."

"Christ, you goddam little"

"Pervert?"

His eyes turned fiercely bright.

"Did you or did you not penetrate her, then, with your penis?"

"No, no, no, no, no."

"Shut your dirty mouth."

"That's what I did."

"*Bit?*"

"No, split the attic and never went back there again and I heard a while later that she was expelled from the school and the principal was discharged and they left town together and a while later my grandmother told me this little girl I played with in her attic had been found dead in some bushes of a park in Tuscaloosa, murdered, my grandmother said, fiendishly molested as your grandfather was, but in bushes, not in a replica of the Blue Grotto."

"You are babbling nonsense."

"No, sir. Maybe I could be elaborating a bit but not fantasizing for your benefit, sir."

Now what I tell you now is fantasy, I think. I think that

I only imagine that when he lifted his flipbook from where his possibly imagined erection had been, there was a liquid stain there. Imagined or not, the consequential thing is that I thought, or imagined, that I now had the ability to excite with words, good and bad, that I was now truly committed to writing which might be, and probably is, despised for its visceral (organic) content.

I saw or I imagined that he had become unstarched and therefore dropped the flipbook back over the unstarched white and scribbled a bit and then said to me, "I have just written my *final* note in your file."

"What is it, please?"

"Arrested at puberty. *Hopeless.*"

⋅•⋅

I saw him no more, and when I recounted to Moise this last interview, the end of which was probably fantasized, she smiled at me and said, "In my opinion, he put the shoe on the wrong foot, dear. People sometimes do."

⋅•⋅

One season I did prevail upon Lance to take me on tour with the ice show. It was the season after my stay at the island resort.

"Sugar, that won't never happen to you again."

"Then take me on tour with you?"

"How would you skate? On your ass?"

"On your back."

"Shit, I got enough monkeys on my back."

But I did prevail, he took me on tour that autumn with the ice show and it resulted in a crescendo of disasters.

The manager of the show was a red-neck from the Texas panhandle with a horror of desegregation.

"Lance, what're you doin' with this white-skin child?"

"This child of God ain't white but an albino."

"Albinos are pink-eyed."

"That is an old wives' tale. This is a genuine young albino which is blue-eyed."

"Show me papers to prove he's an albino nigger befo' he checks in a hotel with you, Lance.'

"Hey, now, Boss-man," said Lance with a touch of derision and threat in his purring voice and cool smile, "since when were nigger albinos given papers to show you? Why, even me, a product of miscegenation as you call it, has no papers to prove it. I got no papers to prove a goddam thing but I prove myself the living nigger on ice when I stop the show every night with a leap and whirl in the air which is the law of gravity defied. You wanta tour without me?"

Lance won that confrontation, but others followed on a rising scale.

Lance and I shared double hotel rooms with another light-skinned black man in the show and with the big black dog that this other black skater insisted on having with him on tour. Somehow the red-neck manager took no exception to this, presumably because the big dog was black and not described as albino.

The black dog and his master were so hung up on each other that the dog kept a sleepless vigil by his owner's bed, breathing quickly and softly through the lengthening nights.

Lance and I slept spoons in our single but it happened

one night in Cleveland, Ohio, that Lance put me on to a pill to make me stop talking in my sleep. And that night I got up to pee and was so disoriented that when I returned from the bathroom I didn't know which bed was ours and turned to the one that wasn't, colliding with the big black dog which instantly bit both my ankles to the bone as if it thought that a little albino like me was about to attack or to rape his master.

Lance sprang up like a shot to see what caused my outcry. Blood was pouring but I was too gone in the head to care about it. However, Lance called in a hotel doctor who stapled the cuts together. I mean he had a metal thing, a stapler, with which he closed the dog-bites on my ankles.

"Shit, this does it, you're flyin' home tomorrow."

But I didn't, I wouldn't, I refused to get out of the cab in which Lance took me to the airport.

"Okay, but, baby, when trouble starts it don't observe a stop sign."

We went on to Sheboygan, me with the staples binding my dog-bites together. And then one night in Sheboygan, when I undressed for bed, I had difficulty in removing my shoes and it was because my ankles were so infected that they had swollen up like an elephant's ankles nearly. Then and not till then did I notice the pain and fever.

"Well, now, li'l blue-eyed albino, I reckon you see why you shouldn't have gone on tour with a fuckin' ice show if you're incapable of seein' anything as visible as your ankles."

Then once again he summoned a hotel doctor, who arrived in a liquefied stupor but nevertheless was impressed by my ankles' swollen condition.

"This boy has a staph infection."

"Is that bad?"

"Bad enough to kill you overnight, so."

He took out of his bag the sort of syringe that I think is only used on horses and filled it with a combination of antibiotics, said, "Drop your drawers," and pumped the contents of the horse-syringe in me.

I felt an almost immediate reaction of a frightening kind. I had such difficulty in drawing my breath that I hobbled to the window and hauled it up. Outside there was a blizzard and I was naked except for my shorts.

"Why're you standing there exposing yourself to that ice storm?"

"So I can breathe, I can't breathe."

(I was into shock from the horse-syringe.)

This sobered up the hotel doctor who snatched up the phone and called an ambulance for me.

Once again I was hauled out of a hotel on a stretcher, by the freight elevator, and shoved into the ambulance waiting downstairs.

Of course Lance accompanied me to the emergency ward, holding hard to my hand, and commanding me to breathe: "In, out, in, out," all the way, and at the hospital's emergency ward I was thrust into a white-curtained cubicle and anti-antibiotics were pumped into me which took three hours to work and in the adjoining cubicles, behind their white curtains, I listened to the life-death struggle of others in much the same condition as I.

I must commend the rapidity with which the interns and nurses rushed about, from cubicle to cubicle, closing and opening curtains. I heard death-cries and I heard sounds of life triumphant.

About four A.M. they declared me out of danger and said that I could be removed to a hospital room upstairs.

Lance followed me up and gently embraced me before a disapproving white nurse.

"Well, sugar, we're doing a matinee tomorrow so I better go catch some sleep."

The nurse made a hmmphing sound of starched disapproval. He turned on her with a slow, deadly grin and said, "You take good care of this young nigger albino."

When he had gone, I inquired of her if I could have a sleeping medication.

"After shock? Are you kidding?"

Well, I got up out of bed and into my clothes. It was painful walking on my elephant ankles down the long corridor to the desk but I got there and said to the bug-eyed receptionist, "Will you please call me a cab."

"This is a hospital, this is not a hotel that you can check out of, you must wait till you are released."

"I am releasing myself."

And while she called for assistance to restrain me, I ran stumbling out into the continuing ice storm and it so happened that God had a cab waiting for me.

(God has cabs as well as sudden subways at his disposal.)

"Take me to the"

For a desperate moment, I couldn't recall the name of the hotel.

"Where?"

I saw two interns rushing out to restrain me and terror shot the name of the hotel into my recollection.

"*Hotel Noble, quick!*"

"*Stop him, he's!*"

"What's your trouble, kid?" the cabbie asked.

I laughed and said, "Love and a dog."

When I got back to the double hotel room, Lance had

zonked himself out and I was received at the door by a very contrite black dog who immediately began to lick at my ankles.

The roommate was awake.

"It's you or the dog," he said.

"You mean?"

"One of you has to go."

"Since the dog is a wolf, or related to the wolf family, why don't you turn it loose in the woods since it's a hazard to mankind?"

"You don't belong to mankind, in my opinion, or the dog's opinion, and the dog could not survive in the woods without me. You got Lance but all I got is the dog."

There was no answer to that.

I crawled into bed and although Lance had never felt warmer or smoother or more protective to touch, I whispered to our roommate,

"Okay, it's me, keep the dog, but occupy a single room with him."

"Singles are hard to come by."

"That I know but I have come by them often."

(Yes, like now, tonight.)

•‣

I stop for a while for breath and I look down at BON AMI.

What is, or rather, what *was* BON AMI? I know it means good friend in French and I remember that when I inquired of Lance soon after I started using it as a work-desk, he said, "Oh, shit, it's some old product that's off the market, I reckon, like you and me are gonna be off it someday." That wasn't all he said. Lance resented BON AMI because he liked his sleep and he claimed the eyeless black domino which was given him by Moise in the days when she could provide such things before she ran out of such things to provide. He claimed that it pressed on his eyeballs and blurred his eyesight. Of course this wasn't the problem. His eyeballs were not the balls to which the domino and BON AMI were an offense. Lance resented BON AMI and the black domino because they interfered with or delayed the rituals of love which were to him an essential for a night's sleep.

"Git your ass off BON AMI and into bed, baby!"

"My ass is not on BON AMI."

"Don't talk back to me, Thelma."

"If you call me Thelma again, I'll"

"You'll what?"

"I'll call you"

"You know better'n to call me nothing with this royal straight pointed at you and you with a single pair."

The talk would go like that, but I am an obstinate writer, as obstinate as unsuccessful, and if Lance persisted in trying to interrupt me when I was hotter for a Blue Jay than even for him, I would run downstairs and continue on the Blue Jay in the Pier Ten bar which used to be across the street from the warehouse but which exists no longer.

(I remember one summer night I did this, and Lance followed me to Pier Ten, he came looming in the door, his bare skin above pants level shining like brass which had just been polished, and everybody looked at him while he looked at me, pretending to be unaware of his entrance. He sat down at the bar and began to talk in ferocious language about me.

"See that prick at the table that thinks he's a writer?"

The barman would utter a low-pitched "*Aw*" and a drunk or two would sometimes turn to look at me at the table and make remarks about me which once incited me to throw a beer mug toward them, but usually, no, the barman would tip them off, if they didn't already know that Lance and I were dangerous to discuss. Lance would go on, though.

"Thinks he's got a literary career but I happen to know that his career is what he is sitting on whenever he's not standing or lying down."

Well, I wasn't afraid of Lance even when he talked in public in this degrading manner. Of course it did stop me writing anything but one phrase over and over in the Blue Jay, and that phrase was "fucking son of a bitch."

Love talk is often rough.

And after a couple of minutes, Lance would come to the table and he would literally pick me up from it and carry me to the warehouse with my Blue Jay and pencil clutched in my fist and

Rough love is appreciation.)

—

(Now I shove BON AMI from me and begin to root around in its interior for more writing surfaces and I find them. Oh, boy, do I find them. You wouldn't think that a big crate like BON AMI had enough space in it to contain all the rejection slips and envelopes they came in which are stashed away inside that box. Although some are mere printed forms to the effect that time does not permit the reading of unsolicited manuscripts, some of them, as I've mentioned before, are graced, so to put it, with those hand-written comments from the editors which I've mentioned before. They appear to be increasingly outraged by the libidinous material of my work, the phrase "sexual hysteria," or something like it, repeatedly surfacing in these put-downs. Miss Sylvia Withers informs me that the world is full of charming subjects for fiction besides the impurely erotic, which is not a preoccupation of *New Humanities Quarterly*. Mr. C. Henry Faulk of *Guard Before Monthly* suggests to me a period of confinement, recommending a monastery in the Great Smoky Mountains where silence and celibacy are practiced.

(Both of these mags are now defunct, ha ha! The laugh is hollow as the bravado of a defeated boxer. Of course I know that I suffer from a chronically inflamed libido and am frequently subject to hysteria. After all, I am Southern with foreskin intact and the organ is somewhat larger than would be proportionate to most male bodies of my size, I still wear shorts with a twenty-eight-inch waist and barely tip the scales at more than one hundred thirty pounds. Lance used to remark, "Baby, I am well hung but you are hung out of sight for a kid that is five foot seven and a fraction or two, and when my heart breaks on ice while your little ticker beats on, I want you to watch it." Watch what did he mean? The consequences of bearing between my thighs a peninsula to my body that, if detached, could pass for a banana approaching maturity though not yet yellowed by the sun? No, I think he meant something of a less material nature, something that had more to do with a future which he feared that I would crash into.)

What is the future of a being with a chronically inflamed libido when the bird of youth has flown out of body and spirit? There's no empyrean into which it ascends like a paraclete. Unless it is corrected or controlled, it could take you to the baths someday and that's where dignity stops and all pretension to it. That is the time of eyes inflamed toward daybreak as the libido, and the haunting of wanting unassuaged by no matter how many mouths. Lance used to tell me about an inscription on the wall of a cubicle in a Boston bath. "Wonderful night of fun. Had ten cocks, took eight biggest up ass." This triumphant inscription on the wall was signed "The Size Queen of Back Bay." No. Repeat no. I would prefer the castration of early death to that sort of future.

A few months ago I ran into a black from Harlem who was into the history of Harlem music and dance from Blues through Jazz and Be-bop and its moods through the wild to the cool and now into the mellow, and he said something that stuck in my mind. "God don't come when you want Him but He's right on time."

Oh, God, I've taken it out of my pants and I'm holding it in my hand and

At home and alone the libido, during these hours, is bound to enter you like an incubus, and if your resistance is down he will control your hand and direct it to where he makes you think you live. You've got to shout to him, "No, I don't live there, not in Place Pig Alley any more than in Sacré Coeur de Montmartre but

Where do you live when alone?

Slowly and sadly, now, I put it back in my jeans and button them up on it as I ask myself that question, "Where do you live when alone?"

In a corner of the dayroom of that asylum on that island in that river to the east?

Words!—don't suffice. . . .

I have just now discovered a very old laundry cardboard, the kind inserted in a laundered shirt, dating from those days when shirts of mine were sent out to be washed and ironed at a laundry no longer existing that was called the Oriental. It is far from an ideal surface for the pencil, having turned darker than its original gray and curling up at the ends and smelling of

I will say it, cockroaches, insects which are so abhorrent to me that I shudder as I

This dates back to the kitchen in Thelma, Alabama, this cockroach phobia of mine. Even in my childhood I associated sleeping alone with death and I would get up barefooted at night to enter the kitchen and before I could reach the light switch there would be that awful crackling and squishing sound underfoot and I'd know I'd stepped on one. That awful content of it, yellow as mucus. I'd sit on the edge of the sink running cold water on the sole of my foot till it was removed, all of it, and I felt clean again.

To be cleansed of defilement is so lovely a thing, and thinking of it, I recall an incident in Thelma when my first symptoms of puberty were appearing, the faint down over the groin and in the armpits, the changed voice, and the penis, rising in sleep, in a dream, to an ecstatic emission of sperm, "the damp initial of Eros," as I once called it in a poem much later.

The incident is this.

A strange limousine had arrived in the city containing four strange young men. No one could fail to notice their elegantly slow drives about the town and the lingering and staring out at male adolescents employed at the stave mill, and Thelma being an innocent town, their reason for this behavior was not suspected correctly. No one knew where they stayed if they stayed anywhere except in the limousine. During the daytime they never rolled down the limousine windows but at night they did to call out in soft voices to youths on the walks. They were there for two days and nights only and it was most commonly rumored of them that they were from Tuscaloosa or Birmingham and were visiting Thelma to attempt to stir up union trouble among the stave mill employees.

On the second night of their stay in Thelma, it was not a stave mill employee but to me that one of the four called out, soft as a dove's voice, from a rapidly rolled-down window of the limousine which was dark as their reputed reason for being in Thelma.

"Son, boy, want a lift where you're going?"

The light of a corner streetlamp shone on his face. He was the blond of the four: I was attracted by the soft voice, the charming intensity of his pale eyes, and simply by the courtesy of the offer of a lift in the handsomest car that I'd even seen in Thelma.

I had been to a Gary Cooper movie at the Bijou and had been so entranced by his face that I'd barely followed the story.

"Why, yes, thanks."

Quickly, silently, the back door of the limousine opened to admit me, and the blond who'd spoken to me lifted me across his knees to the space between him and a sculpturally motionless young man with equally intense-looking eyes.

No sooner than I was sitting between the blond and the dark than the window was raised and the limousine purred into motion.

The blond did all the talking at first.

"Where are you going, boy?"

"Home."

"Where's that?"

"The corner of Cherry and Peach Street."

As I mentioned this location of home, someone in the front seat broke into laughter which all of the four occupants of the limousine echoed a bit. It was a private joke among them, it would seem, the street-names of the corner I lived on.

"How old are you, boy?"

"Fourteen."

"Aren't you scared to be in a car with four men you don't know?"

I began to shiver at this question, especially since it was accompanied by a hand of the dark man and a hand of the blond each falling rather tightly onto my knees as if I were being taken a prisoner between them.

But I answered,

"No, why should I be?"

"A pretty young boy like you?"

"I don't understand what you mean but I'd like to get out now."

In response the limousine picked up speed and not in the direction of my home but out into dark open country.

"You're not driving toward Peach and Cherry."

Again the chorus of laughter. The blond laughed softest and said, "Have a little fresh country air with us first."

"No, no, I want to get out."

By this time I was scared crazy, for the limousine and the mysterious four were out into dark moonless country and the hands of each beside me had advanced from my knees to my upper thighs and were rhythmically squeezing as women shoppers do melons to see if they're ripe.

And now the blond's had closed gently over my groin and he inquired, "Doesn't this feel good?"

Whether it did or didn't, I was too frightened to answer.

Then abruptly the limousine stopped and the dark one seized my hand and placed it in his lap and held it there tightly and I felt his large erection, and then it was he that spoke.

"Get his pants off him, undress him, let's give him instruction."

"Such as what?" asked the blond in a suddenly harsh, reproving voice.

"How to suck and."

"Listen, bitch," said the blond, "this boy is only a child and we're driving him straight home to Peach and Cherry. Come here, boy. Sit in my lap. Don't let that bastard touch you."

He lifted me onto his knees and opened them wider and held me tight between them.

Apparently he had the power among them, for the limousine started again and turned about toward the town.

The blond also had an erection but made no suggestions to me, just held me protectively between his tight thighs.

The limousine lurched to a stop at Peach and Cherry. There was a moment of stillness. The blond had inserted his hand inside my white shirt.

"His heart's beating like a wild bird."

"Get him out," said the dark one.

The door on the blond's side opened, his thighs released

me, and as I got up to get out, I felt his hand on my ass, not squeezing but caressing, and he said to the dark one, "It would have been lovely if you hadn't fucked it up."

"Nobody's fucked nothing."

"Not yet," said the blond, "but you're going to sit on my cock all the way back to Mobile and I hope the road is bumpy."

I didn't step out of the limousine but fell out.

The blond leaned out the window.

"Are you okay, baby?"

I got to my feet. The blond was still leaning his beautiful head out the window.

It was I that kissed him, a soft, lingering kiss.

"Take care, take care," he whispered, and the limousine drove away.

—

Thinking back upon that adventure, now sixteen years past, I have a feeling that those four strangers have gone further than Mobile through a night much deeper. There was about them an atmosphere of death on the invisible road map of existence not far along it despite the fact that the driver of the limousine, whose dark head never turned toward me, drove with an exceptional skill and ease as if he were a part of the machine, a controlling extension of it, one that owned a commanding block of units in the stock of a corporation, the limousine, although I am sure it was actually the property of the blond one. But death. It did seem to have been written in disappearing ink on each of their individual road maps of existence at separate little distances, four deaths like a cluster of darkly luminous dials which I glimpsed on the dashboard, and I believe that this feeling belongs in the realm of the parapsychological in which I've grown to have total faith.

When there is one of a thing there is likely to be another or even two more and I have discovered a second laundry cardboard a bit further under the bed than was the first, whose writing surfaces are now covered. I reduce the size of my penciling to a point at which it will be legible only to myself so that this barricade of words against loneliness can be longer maintained.

Of the four young men who drove away to Mobile and my intuition of their lives being completed not long after they left Thelma, I have only one more thing to confess in my relation to them and it is that I would like to have held the blond one in my arms, over my lap, at the time of his passing. This is an erotic feeling, needless to tell you. I would like to have felt the spasmodic motions of his prone body as it surrendered its warmth of being and to have placed one hand on his forehead and the other over his groin to comfort him at the two places where he lived most intensely and would have most resisted ravishment by the non-living, by the mineral kingdom.

Certainly not all nor most of my adventures in Thelma, Alabama, were of the sort that seem inclined to surface on the currents of my unconscious tonight. What I am doing tonight is what I have done all nights that I've spent alone in this space flimsily partitioned from a much, much larger and darker space that inevitably reminds me of the unmentionable which I keep mentioning which is the vastness of the nothing, the nowhere, out of which emerges the momentary light-flicker of being alive and drops back into it so precipitately, even in lingering cases, with the miraculous swoop of an aerialist at the top of a circus tent, swinging between a pair of trapezes with no net beneath him. It is the act, the moment of brilliance: and then the failure to fly, the plummeting out of light to the heart of the black, with no great public gasp of terror and dismay that is comparable to that which occurs in his heart as he finds that he has miscalculated his leap at the cost of his being.

Oh, God, what am I doing with this affectation of a style like Pierre Loti's at the century's turn?

I was saying that I'm doing tonight what I have done every night when alone since entering the "broken world of love" except that I am not naked in bed and turned upon my stomach to press the warmth of my half-tumescent prick against the space deserted by Lance on tour.

"Baby, you want to write but you got no education," he said to me once, annoyed that I remained seated at BON AMI with Blue Jay, pencil scribbling, instead of coming to bed.

"You mean formal education, no adequate schooling, you mean."

"Baby, you got less than I got."

"How do you know?"

"Shit, the truant officer was hot on your heels when I met you."

"Only according to Mama, a mythologist of the first order. Actually in Thelma, Alabama, I got about as much schooling as the poet Arthur Rimbaud got in Charleville when he grabbed the school prize and quit."

"What cat is that?"

"If you don't know, you better not brag about your education."

"Shit, when I met you, you were certainly listed by the Bureau of Missing Persons."

"Yes, and I still am."

"Baby, ain't you well-fucked? The answer to that is yes, not no, and so if you're missing, you are not missing much."

"I would like to be something more permanent than a receptacle for sperm which is sometimes infected with germ cells by anonymous donors you encounter at midnight on tour with an ice show."

"Don't sit there talking to me like a little library queen."

"Don't lie there talking to me like a hustler that gives it away for residence in this godforsaken pad."

"If you don't like my life-style"

"Do *you*?"

"A man's life-style should fit his future more than his present, and in my future I won't be the star of the ice show, I will not be the living nigger on ice forever, baby, but I will be a junkie and this pad here will be appropriate to my condition then."

"I don't contest the point since I know your habits, but how about me, should I adjust my life to the future of a"

"Nigger junkie?"

"You said it, man, not me."

"The red-neck is coming out in you, and lemme warn you, it brings out the hellcat in me."

"You've got hazel-speckled green eyes like a fire-cat, Lance, you burned your way into my life and you'll burn yourself out and I will be left burned-out behind you like a village of thatch-roof huts that you've set fire to and sacked and ravaged and *don't!*"

He was trying to haul me off the box onto the bed and I knew it would be not for love but for revenge.

"This could be our last communion," he warned me, and his hand slackened its hold.

"Yes, without any sacrament to it."

"Okay, let's lighten it up. Tell me more about your self-education in Thelma, baby."

I drew a long breath before resuming our talk, which turned out to be our last one, and then I said evenly as I could with his fire-cat eyes burning holes through my bare back, "In Thelma I went every evening to the public library which was endowed by a wealthy old widow and contained all the classics translated from the Greeks to the young poet Rimaud whom I resemble."

"How do I know what he looked like, you or not?"

"Because," and I snatched out a page removed from a Thelma, Alabama, library book which was the famous portrait of Rimbaud when he'd first come to Paris and was seated among the Paris literati of that day in the picture *Au Coin de la Table.*

"Is this you, baby?"

"See, it almost could be, but it's the poet Rimbaud and I tore it out of a Thelma, Alabama, library book about him. I had to do it secretly so I went into the stacks which I had permission to enter and I coughed very loud to cover up the sound of tearing it out."

"So you were a little library queen in Thelma who ripped off pictures from books and that makes you educated enough to be a New Yawk writer, is that the pitch?"

"That is the truth, not a pitch. Oh, I never got into trigonometry or Plato's discourses in Greek, but as a writer, I am not handicapped by illiteracy as you think."

His large hot hand caught roughly hold of my shoulder and he jerked me off BON AMI onto the bed.

"You are turning me off with this literary shit."

He leaned very tall from the bed to blow out the kerosene lamp by which I wrote on BON AMI and by which I'm still writing on it.

"I wish you'd pursue your literary career when I'm pursuing mine on ice which is not literary."

◆

In this I return to the confession that few of my adventures or experiences in Thelma were of a precociously erotic kind.

I did, indeed, go every evening to the Thelma public library and by the age of ten I had read all of Shakespeare, for instance, in preference to Edgar Rice Burroughs' Tarzans and the Fu Manchu books.

"Good evening, little prodigy," was the greeting which I received from the lady librarian, sarcastic, I suppose.

It may be pertinent to my character that I preferred *Titus Andronicus* to *Hamlet,* and almost to *Othello* and *Macbeth.*

Reading it, I had to laugh at the outrageous excess of the Queen of the Goths being served up a meat pie at a banquet, and the meat being the flesh of her two sons who had ravished Lavinia.

(I suppose that writers are predisposed to laugh at all excesses but their own.)

Then there were the retired minister and his wife, the Reverend and Mrs. Lakeland, who were trying to survive on a sub-subsistence level and yet who sat on their gray porch as tranquilly as if their lives contained no trials at all. And yet they sat there with their chair-arms touching, he in his rusty-looking clerical suit with freshly starched round collar and she in a clean white dress with yellow polka dots on it as faint as the dabs of color on Moise's final (?) canvas. And it was rumored, too, that she was wasting away from an internal illness of a painful nature but would take no morphine for it because morphine cost more than they could afford and they were too proud or something to accept it without charge.

"Good evening, Reverend Lakeland, how are you, Mrs. Lakeland?"

"Fine, thank you, we're just fine. And how are you all doing?"

I would hear this periodically all late summer afternoons in Thelma since they lived in the house next door.

Their voices were lifted with a valiant effort.

Still they declined to accept, or rather to keep, the baskets of provisions that were sometimes placed anonymously at their door. The Reverend Lakeland would pass these charities along to a cotton-topped black man, even older than the Reverend, who would drop by now and then.

"Good evening, Mr. Lyndon."

"Good evening, Reverend, how you, Mrs. Lakeland?"

"Oh, we're fine, just fine. Would you be good enough to remove this basket of"

By this time the cotton-topped black would be on the porch and their voices would drop to those inaudible whispers which they exchanged between themselves while looking out from their chairs at the approach of dark.

Sitting on our porch adjoining theirs one evening, I inquired of Mother,

"What are they like, Mother?"

"They're eccentric."

My grandmother laughed, softly and mockingly.

"So's your son, that doesn't answer his question."

"Please, let's drop the subject."

"When've you ever done anything else with a subject?" her mother muttered in a rebellious tone.

"Son, help your grandmother inside and make her some cocoa."

"I don't need help inside or cocoa made for me. Listen, son. You know what an insult is and that's what they have received, they've received an intolerable insult from the Bishop of the Diocese and from the town of Thelma. Why else do you think they sit out there except in defiance of people passing by who delivered this intolerable insult to them and think they can rectify it with the baskets left at their door after they've gone inside, and him rejecting morphine for his wife's pain, intolerable as the insult from the church and town of Thelma?"

"*Mother*," said Mother, rising abruptly from her wicker rocker and jerking the screen door open.

My grandmother let her stand there while she studied the night sky for a minute or two, then rose indifferently to enter the house.

"Intolerable insult it was and you may not explain what it was concerning the Lakelands but he will discover the meaning concerning himself and I hope he responds to it as quietly and fiercely as they do."

She entered the house then, grandly, an old tigress.

My interest in the Reverend and Mrs. Lakeland was now aroused to a point that demanded more complete information and I soon hit upon a likely source of it in the person of a dyed redhead named Pinkie Sales, a lady whose hair had been flaming in her youth and which remained flaming at sixty by benefit of bottled products from the drugstore.

She moved briskly about the block at practically the same blue hour of dusk every evening, talking to her chained companion, a poodle red-eyed as a drunk. Somehow the two of them had the theatrical effect of a parade with a band although the band was Pinkie's high-pitched whisper and an occasional little recalcitrant yap from the poodle.

"Will you come along now, quit sniffing and pissing, you're not going to promenade the streets all night."

So I thought to myself, if she'll talk to that drunk-eyed poodle she will talk to me, so I fell in step with her one evening and after polite "Good evenings," I said to her, "I wonder if you can tell me about the ex-Reverend that lives next door to us, Miss Pinkie."

"Oh, sonny, I don't think I should discuss it, it's too awful and you're too young."

"I just want to know if they received an intolerable insult from the Bishop and Thelma and what kind of insult it was."

"All right, dear, help me get Belle to the drugstore and promise not to repeat a thing I say about the Reverend Lakeland and I'll tell what I know. They had a daughter, you know, that used to scream out the window and one time the Bishop was having dinner with them and the daughter appeared at the table, fetching a chair to the table directly across from him."

"Oh. Did she scream?"

"No, but she threw the chicken in his face."

"Just that?"

"Lord, sonny, that was sufficient on top of the Reverend Lakeland's heretical opinions of the Bible. He insisted that the Old Testament was a lot of fairy tales that contained too many characters engaged in incestuous relations, the congregation wasn't at all pleased by it and the

Bishop wasn't either and the chicken was so tough he had trouble with it. Then the daughter screamed at him and threw a drumstick into his face which was dripping with gravy. Lah, lah, lah, said the Lakelands, trying to swab the gravy off him. But it did no good at all. 'Put your daughter away and recant these heresies from the pulpit next Sunday or you will be removed without pension and God help your souls, good evening.' And the Bishop stalked out and that next Sunday the Reverend Mr. Lakeland made two sermons, one about the flight of his daughter to places unknown and the second about his confirmed opinion that the Old Testament was the most unbelievable document ever put in print. Well, that did it. Out without pension, and I hear without a trace of their wildcat daughter. How people go out in this world, well, here's the drugstore, good evening."

She tugged at Belle, who yapped, and went clicking on her spike heels to the cosmetics counter and said loudly to the clerk, "Henna, please, and Shalimar perfume, will you shut up, Belle?"

A few days before I left Thelma, Alabama, Mrs. Lakeland at last succumbed to her illness, and that night their house went up in flames, cremating them both: a pair of old human boards, dove-jointed, on which perched love and madness as two inseparable specters. The hoses of the fire department were mostly turned on our house to protect it from the contagion of flame and heresies, and the scandal of the fugitive daughter. The fugitive impulse ran very strong in the sons and daughters of Thelma, just as strongly as the hanging-on impulse ran in the slowed-down blood of their fathers and mothers.

So many *good evenings* in Thelma.

And here the cat-pack kisses and the *Bon soir, Désespoir,*

in so many hearts at this hour, oh, but on we go with it to the end of our Blue Jays, except for those having the valor of the Reverend Mr. Lakeland the night that he was alone and driven to arson and the final heresy of self-destruction.

(Their bodies were committed to unhallowed ground.)

And I think it is time now for me to write "quoth the raven" or to slip through the corner crevice of the plywood enclosure to see how the long night continues.

⬦

What I actually did was to go into the bathroom to look at my face in the small, square mirror attached with adhesive tape to the wall above the washbasin, a thing that I do at times when I have a feeling of being unreal: *not* to assure myself that, unlike a vampire, I am reflected by glass: and while I was in there trying to face myself as a visible and believable creature, I heard footsteps on the staircase from West Eleventh. Naturally I assumed that it was Charlie returning. My heart did things in my chest like a waking bird. I leaned very close to the bit of mirror to see if my face could be suitably prepared to face my wayward lover, but what I saw was a face that suggested that of a character in a silent film revival, frothing and spitting with rage, a close-up that belonged over a caption such as: "How dare you face me again?" I stood there counting to ten and attempting to erase these facial contortions and replace them with a look of haughty indifference, if such a look exists in the range of expressions, when the person who had trudged stumblingly up the staircase spoke out in a voice that was husky with drink and much lower pitched than Charlie's could ever be. The voice was familiar to me, not from long acquaintance but from very recent encounter: still I couldn't place it.

"So you're a writer, too," was what the voice said.

Then I knew who it was and I came out of the bathroom and there, indeed, was the freakish old playwright attempting a comeback at the Truck and Warehouse Theater by the Bowery. He was seated on the bed leafing through the last of my Blue Jays. He must have known that I was observing this outrageous invasion of my—about writing, can you say privacy? No, but still, to root through a writer's work without invitation is the height of insolence. He laid the Blue Jay aside, still not looking up at me, and squinted his good eye at an Oriental cardboard and at a large rejection envelope. He looked sad but unembarrassed. I cleared my throat. I shifted my weight from one foot to another. He continued squinting and reading.

At last I broke the silence with something verbal.

"Is it your custom to go through the unpublished writings of strangers without permission? And is it your custom to invade their bedrooms at any hour of night simply because"

"Because of what?" he asked in that voice which was nearly as ravaged as his vision.

"Because they don't have a door locked against intruders?"

"Proprieties are properties I've forgotten through"

"Through what?"

"Through desperation, which is a product of time you haven't had time to explore."

"How would you know I haven't?"

"I don't see well. Anyway, to have mentioned desperation

would have been a tasteless appeal for sympathy which—
I was about to say I don't want, and that would be shit,
too."

"Well, you've said it, by intention or not. You know,
under some conditions I might feel sympathy for you but
they're not conditions that prevail on me now. You look
to me like an old con man, playing words instead of the
pigeon drop or poker with a stacked deck."

"That's very odd what you said, the pigeon drop. You
know, a couple of years ago I was sailing for Europe because at the time I thought a transatlantic plane flight would
give me another coronary, and the day before sailing I'd had
a furious confrontation with my publishers' secretary over
the phone. I'd learned they were planning to bring out
several volumes of my plays under the title *The Collected
Works of*. So I called them up and got this secretary and I
told her that I would not accept that title, *Collected Works*,
since I was not yet certain my work was finished and I said
to her, 'Tell them that I suggest this alternate title, *The
Pigeon Drop*,' and I told her what it was, that it was a
con game which is played on a senile mark with savings
in the bank. Won't bore you with the details, perhaps you
know them. But at dinner the first night out I received
a ship-to-shore call from one of the publishers and he
assured me that they didn't regard my work as a con game
and that if I objected to *The Collected Works*, how about
using *The Theater of* instead."

He fell silent then.

"Is that all?"

"Well, I believe in peaceful concessions, so I settled for
The Theater of, although it struck me as pretentious and"

"You believe in unfinished sentences, too."

"You don't sound like you want me to go on."

"No, I got the point. Would you mind moving over on the bed."

He moved over slightly.

"A little more than that slightly."

"Do you think I've come here with seduction in mind?"

"In a world of infinite jeopardy, why take chances you can avoid?"

"Can you?"

He had now moved to the other end of the bed so I sat down.

"Get your smart ass off my pillow, please."

He put the pillow behind him and leaned back.

"I went back to my hotel but I couldn't go in alone. I've tried to return alone to a lot of hotels at night lately and it's more and more dreadful. I've taken to asking bellhops and elevator boys when they get off duty, and if it's before daybreak I beg them to come to my room and I wait up till I'm sure they're not going to show before I try to sleep. Oh. Something funny. A few nights ago one of them did show before daybreak, enticed by the promise of a large compensation for his service which is only to hold me till the Nembutal works, just to hold me, I swear. Oh, preferably unclothed but not necessarily so. Well, this one did show. I was in one of my two Sulka robes and asked him to put on the other but he declined, just sat in a straight-back chair by the bed and said, 'Drop it, the Nembie, I ain't got all day.' So I dropped it and washed it down with a glass of wine and all at once as my sight blurred with sedation I saw him as the film actor Dalessandro. I gasped and said to him, 'Hold me, hold me.' I had my arms extended. And what he did was to take hold of one of my hands in a gingerly fashion as if he suspected I had some awful contagion communicable by touch. Isn't that funny?"

"No, I don't find it any more amusing than did the bell-hop or"

"Elevator boy," he prompted. "But, you see, that same evening when he'd let me off at the tenth floor, he had the impertinence to say to me, 'Watch your step, Miss.'"

"You should be flattered that he didn't say 'Madam.'"

"You're being a little bitchy, but I don't mind. I believe it's indigenous to this part of the city."

"It's what you get for slumming."

"Baby, I'm not slumming even on Boogie Street in Singapore where cockroaches fly in your face after midnight but they've got the most beautiful transvestites in the world, more feminine than women, I swear it's true."

"I didn't question the fact but I wish you'd stop messing around with my manuscripts like I'd submitted them to you."

"Sorry. I'm not quite conscious. Are you at all interested in foreign travel?"

"You asked me that before. The answer was negative and it's still the same, maybe more so."

"It wouldn't involve more than occupying an adjoining room, answering phones and helping me with carry-on plane luggage. Oh, and sitting with me at lunch and dinner. You see, I can stand sleeping alone but not eating and drinking alone."

"I should think by your age you'd have learned that you have to stand a lot of things you can't stand."

"Yes, including myself. I remember once the host on a TV talk show said to me, 'Do you like yourself?' to which

I responded with a blank look and a silence and then he said, 'Do you *adore* yourself?' and I said, finally, 'Well, I am stuck with myself and have to put up with it as best I can.' So you don't like foreign travel?"

I could see that he was no longer listening even to himself.

When he wasn't talking he was almost, I mean he would have been almost, a bearable presence. But how long does a creature like this stop talking while still partially living? I realized he was right when he had called me bitchy, partially right as he was now partially conscious. After all, his effrontery was enormous. But on the other hand perhaps his loneliness corresponded to it in size. I was now able to observe him more objectively. I saw that he was about my height and, Christ, yes, the Cyclops eye was about the same color as my eyes were and I had always regarded them as my best facial feature, a sort of light lettuce green. In his case, however, there was chronic inflammation and the lightness might be symptomatic of a cataract developing on the good eye, too. And the mouth hung open slightly in an unpleasant way. The nose was regular but the nostrils slightly distended and veined. He had unbuttoned but not removed the fur coat. Probably once he'd had a neat build but that was once, not now, he was now a pretty good model for a painter with a hang-up on spheres. And how could I be sure, intentions false or true, that under the influence of two bottles of wine and perhaps a barbiturate he mightn't come through that door to the adjoining room, unclothed or in a Sulka robe, and cry out, "Hold me, hold me!" Did I like foreign travel that much? Was I that much of a hustler, which I had never been in my life? No, I remarked emphatically, and I must have said it out loud since his eye focused on me again and he blinked it so that a streak of liquid rolled down the cheek on that side.

"No what?"

"I don't like foreign travel."

"Oh, but you might acquire a taste for it, especially by first class, jumbo jet, there's really a lot to be said for coming out of the clouds over Hong Kong at night, all of that gorgeously tacky neon in ideograms you can't read, so you can imagine they're advertisements of the sensual allurements and satisfactions of the whole Orient, if you have yellow fever and a taste for buttocks that are smooth as breasts, and there are still several old hotels in the traditional style that haven't gone to seed such as the Royal Hawaiian, very high ceilings and revolving fans, and the Hotel Mena in Cairo is in sight of the pyramids, a very short ride by camel, and in Bangkok you can occupy the suite that was occupied by Somerset Maugham and Noel Coward or you can move to the modern high-rise annex that's air-conditioned, sometimes comfort has to take precedence over esthetics in the Far East. Tokyo's out for me because of the air pollution but I had an unforgettable cab ride with a Japanese youth like a pale yellow rose after I'd collapsed at his feet somewhere along the Ginza, all the way to Yokohama, I recovered halfway there and to distract myself from the warning of mortality on the Ginza, I'd placed a hand on his thigh and he had actually moved it like a chess piece to his crotch and put his hand on mine. . . ."

"Well, somebody was overplaying his hand."

"Somebody always does that. I don't know if it's the human comedy or tragedy, but sometimes there's a bit of humanity in it. Do you like foreign travel, I mean could you bear it with me?"

"Maybe five years from now if we're alive."

(I nearly added, "and you're immobilized and finally speechless.")

I was rather shocked by the cruelty of my attitude toward this derelict who had stumbled into my life some hours before, shouting—what was it he'd shouted as he crashed out of the Truck and Warehouse lobby? Something about it being too dreadful to believe? He wasn't speaking to me then and so it wasn't a pitch for sympathy at that point. What troubled me was my lack of sympathy now that I'd come to know him. To lack sympathy for the unknown, reported on a newscast as having been burned alive in a nursing home fire, well, that's inaccurate, you feel sympathy, you may even feel a vicarious horror, but the next minute you're laughing at a close-up of Nixon and Brezhnev at a banquet in a fifteenth-century palace in the Kremlin, but this icy revulsion I felt for the man who only had the enticements of luxurious foreign travel to offer me in exchange for his intrusion on what was an existence almost as derelict as his own, a difference only in years, wasn't it an ominous sign in someone who wanted to write? Couldn't it mean that I was already too old for my chosen vocation? Jet-aged by Charlie's defection? Or could the revulsion be for—

There are some sentences that a distinguished failed writer must be ashamed to complete, as if telling a secret which has been publicly published in yesterday's paper. I drew a long and loud breath which reminded me of the respirations of the Queen of Tragedy while reading the Psalms at that long-ago posh party uptown, it was breath enough to have lifted a black kite toward the sky, but all it produced was the terribly ordinary and suspect statement that follows.

"You're trying to buy me and I'm not for sale."

I looked at him once more and, oh, God, saw again that portrait of myself which had aged like St. Oscar's boy Dorian.

Enough self-loathing, sometimes a form of self-pity: I knew by this time that he would not be frustrated even by double doors locked between adjoining rooms, no, he would phone the bell captain and request, in a husky whisper, that the doors be unlocked between us, and I, well, in a world so full of whores too hungry to refuse any offer, why should he pick on me?

Then he resumed our dialogue with a single word of one letter, he said "*I*," and that seemed to bring into instantly sharp focus the reason for my revulsion, and I took instant advantage of it by saying, "Yes, you, you, you, interminably *you*, isn't that your problem?"

"Isn't it yours, too?"

"No, I'm concerned with some others."

"And you think I'm not? Do you think it was easy getting back here in another cab with a very impatient cabbie and no address to give him but West Eleventh and the smell of the river?"

"But your motive in making this effort was not at all limited to? Oh, yesterday I encountered a word I'd never heard before. It was "solipsism." I looked it up in Webster's

Unabridged at the library and it said something to the effect that it meant to live exclusively in and for yourself. Want me to write it down for you? Give me a slip of paper from your wallet."

"I know the word as well as I know my name."

Now both of us were staring straight ahead and breathing like spent runners. I felt that I was already out of his presence though still bodily in it. I only needed a few words more which he supplied, along with a light touch on my knee.

"Oh, my dear boy."

"Excuse me while I check the other room."

(I sprang up.)

"I think maybe my lover has returned by the back entrance."

"If he'd returned and hadn't bothered to come in to kiss you good night or explain his long absence, isn't he a mistake?"

"He might be ashamed to face me or to interrupt this intense dialogue between us, and anyway, I prefer him to foreign travel."

"I remember. Designed by Praxiteles, or cunningly copied from the master by an apprentice. I know what people say, salacious, decadent, prurient, shameless, I've had the whole crock thrown at me but still keep going, and as for your preference, I accept it, very reluctantly but with understanding. Yesterday I was checking through my address books and had to cross out a lot of names and numbers that were victims of time, so many that I'm inconsolable and nearly scared to death, and *that* is *solipsism*."

"I think you'd better accept it."

"It's unacceptable."

"That's another misapprehension of yours, the solipsism of your life is going to contain the solipsism of your death, and if you're not out of this room when I come back, I will somehow manage to get you an ambulance to Bellevue."

I was on my feet but not moving and for some reason which I don't know, or prefer not to know, I was quivering as if a fierce electric current was circuited through my nerves, yes, I believe it was the equivalent of EST on the island in the East River.

Then fantasy really took over. I didn't turn my head toward him to look at him again but my head pivoted that way and so did my eyes and what I saw was an old man smiling, a very old child smiling at me wisely.

He nodded at me, then moved back to the position on the bed that faced BON AMI and began to write on a piece of hotel stationery and I don't think he noticed it when I went back through the crevice in the rectangle as if there actually were another humanly habitable room in the warehouse where Charlie might be waiting.

Oh, I suspect that when I read this over I will scrap the whole bit about the derelict's return to the derelict. . . .

＊

How strange to find myself up here at this uncertain hour, on the roof of the abandoned warehouse, six empty floors above that little improvised human shelter I have occupied with an implausible sense of security, persisting against all reason, through fifteen years and two loves. I do not use exclamation marks as I think that they are probably the most dispensable piece of punctuation to which a writer can descend unless he is writing for dumb actors and actresses like that unfortunate playwright whom I encountered before the Truck and Warehouse Theater. I suppose it may be necessary to indicate to the less gifted members of the acting profession that a line is to be shouted or spoken in a tone of shock or fury by following it with that despicable bit of punctuation. As for a distinguished failed prose writer, surely he can content himself with the comma and the period and the marks for quotation of speech between persons and also, in my peculiar case, with the neat spaces which indicate the division of section from following section as a slight variation indicates the progression of a fugue in the world of music.

Now how did I manage to get up here on the roof of the warehouse since there is no means of elevation but wings, if I had them, or such mechanical contrivances for moving upward as the escalator or the elevator, neither of which exists in operative condition in the building's vast darkness.

Having spoken of dark, let me speak now of light. I have come up by long flights of stairs to the roof of the building, I am actually on the roof of it, and I find that the roof is much lighter than I had imagined it could be. It is light enough for me to sit here on a ledge above dockside West Eleventh and continue to write and to see what I'm writing if I write in bolder script with more pressure on the pencil as I am doing.

My heartbeat is quickened by the climb through the six dark, unoccupied floors, and sometimes I feel a premature or delayed contraction of that defective heart valve which Grandmother Ursula Phillips claimed that I had inherited from the Phillipses of Kentucky but which I think more likely to have been a consequence of one of those childhood illnesses so rarely diagnosed by small-town Southern doctors as rheumatic fever (or break-bone fever if the child is colored), and let go at that without informed treatment.

(I know that I had a long spell of illness at eight or nine which interrupted my schooling for a year and turned me to solitary diversions such as reading and fantasizing, and when the bedridden period was over my legs were weakened so that I slid on my ass about the floor and was given a child's vehicle called an "Irish Mail," a three-wheeled thing that was propelled by pushing its handlebars back and forth, and I remember my first time outside on it I got as far as half a block and was suddenly exhausted and had nothing to lean back against and so began to cry, slumped over the handlebars, until my mother, who had watched me from a window, came rushing up to me and pushed me home on the thing and carried me into the house and said I mustn't go out again on it, but I was as stubborn as the damaged valve of my heart and went out on it again, despite her hysterical protests, and each time went a bit further on it until I could make a full turn about the block.)

While my heart slowly resumes a more natural pace, I think, "Well, so you are closer to eternity (that euphemism for lasting blackout) than most men are at thirty but you get about now without the Irish Mail, and anyhow, being bereft of your second love and a third one being inconceivable to you, why should you hang back at the turnstile of the subway?"

(Isn't there a subway station called *Far Rockaway?*)

◆

Sitting on the ledge of the warehouse roof with my legs dangling in air as casually as if I were seated on a fan-

134

tastically tall chair, quite unsuitably clothed for the icy night, I know that I'm shivering but I don't feel cold. And I know this illusory warmth is that of fever (in which case the word "illusory" should be scratched out) or of an artificial state of mind induced by a white cross and quickened bloodstream and, whatever it is, I am indifferent to it as if it belonged to a stranger I've never seen.

Now back to the subject of light.

Some of it must come from the far-apart river-fogged streetlamps or even from a few windows across the way, lighted by monkish scholars or for love-partners who like to watch each other strip for action, but I suspect that it also emanates from the sky despite the fact that it is clouded or fogged over.

Moise called me "child of God," a flattering appellation (when will He ever get into birth control?) and I am just high enough on this warehouse roof and that reliquary white cross to recognize this as a time for purification of my forsaken and ailing body by thoughts upon the absolutes of existence, and on the non of it before it occurs and after.

It's true that I feel something mystical on this rooftop.

Looking up from it, I observe little areas of lesser dark, almost of light, as if a number of clouded moons were suspended up there with that attention to "plastic space" which Moise observes in her distribution of slightly lighter or darker dabs of pigment when she has pigments to dab. She does it with great concentration, that of a chess player in a master tournament, and speaking of plastic space, I recall that, when I first knew her, she used that term in reference to a canvas which she had titled "Northern Limit of Ice Floe." This was before I knew her well and at a time when I wished to impress Lance with my intellectual

1 3 5

capacity, such as it was not, and when I was in the first full passion of that great love which must always include the ignoble element of unwillingness to share the object of it. And so I said, "I know what plastic means and of course I know what space means but what the fuck do they mean when you put them together in a term like plastic space?"

"Hey, li'l bit of white skin," said the living nigger on ice, "just set there with your pretty teeth in your mouth without words when Moise discusses her work, or otherwise you'll make a li'l bit of Thelma, Alabama, asshole of yourself cause this girl here knows what she says although she rarely says it."

"Then what is plastic space?" I persisted bristling with

"Let me inform him," she whispered. "On a canvas there is always space and the space must be as plastic as the paint and you will notice that I always begin a canvas by covering it entirely with an off-white or off-black layer of pigment for beginning. Now this is space. And the space is plastic. Which means that it is as vibrantly alive as the dabs of paint applied so carefully to it. Space is alive, not empty and dead, not at all just a background. It's as much a part of the living canvas as the bits of color. As the student of Hans Hoffman, this mystery was made clear, the meaning and the importance of plastic space."

She went on speaking but her voice had dropped below the decibel of the audible but her lips moved and her eyes were brilliant and I was so impressed that I

Lance drew me almost painfully close into his arms with his fingers on the lips of Moise, which was when I discovered that through their attachment he had learned the art of lip-reading by touch. . . .

The white cross has inclined me to long tangents of this nature but now I drift into consideration of the absolutes of existence as a paper kite at a time of listless air motion will catch just enough of the air to lift it a few feet over the earth or your head before dropping it back down as if it had found it unworthy of levitation.

"The absolutes of existence" is surely a much more pretentious term than "plastic space," but back of their appearance of pretension there is important meaning if you want to sustain an existence above the surface of day-to-day and night-to-night submission to just going on. You consider them if you don't want that, and especially if you're alone, waiting to know if aloneness is not a life term that's been imposed on you but subject to clemency.

It's difficult, though, to consider those absolutes, even with flu fever and a white cross in you and the night sky above, and the more you consider them the larger they become and the less penetrable to the workings of that bewildered top-piece above the majority of your "li'l bit of white skin" which I think he really meant was penetrable white flesh, it being more flesh that he valued than the skin and its color.

Absolutes are deferred in our contemplation and understanding, they just peek through them as eyes in heaven, perhaps.

These absolutes (which are God) say to us, "Your payment is deferred till"

"When?"

"Till I choose to be known to you."

"After death?"

No answer.

And so I think, "Arrogant old Absolutes" or, "Conceited Mr. E.," which is my name for God.

But this is only a moment of anger at them and you return to the purifying spectacle of the night sky which is overcast but oddly lighter in places like blurred moons or dabs of paint in plastic space.

Your fever and the white cross lift you above the pettiness of your annoyance at what you can't know, now or possibly ever.

And so I look toward Bleecker Street where Moise announced her retirement from the world of reason which she mistakenly supposed to be outside of her room and corridor and her door without address and where she made her probably unheeded appeal to the bearded seer of South Orange, and where this announcement and this appeal were repeated with slight variation to the accompaniment of the delirious hissing of Skates and her attendant bitches. I looked that way and observed that it was no longer night. It is a winter phenomenon of the lower, the dockside, Hudson that morning hardly intrudes upon early morning. Streetlamps are extinguished as if the sun's light were present but what is present is the faintest concession to gray and

A sudden and very violent fit of shivers has sent me scurrying down those never-before-discovered stairs to the warehouse roof. On the way I descended at intervals on my ass and my Phillips of Kentucky heart performed several lickety-split palpitations but none of this mattered at all. It wasn't noticeable to me. Nothing short of a broken pelvis would have been noticeable to me, or a coronary such as my maternal grandfather suffered in the replica of the Blue Grotto in the replica of the new Babylon, or, more pertinent as an appellation, the new Sodom, oh, but to refer to it as that would bring down on my cracked head the wrath of all the Gay Libs to whom my heart is committed, categorically, in a bruised-ass way. . . .

A bruised-ass way is surely a half-ass way and yet I know that I am in favor of all conceivable libs this side of My Lai and of child-molesters in public.

Well, I had returned to the hooked rectangle, panting and palpitating and still shivering from rooftop exposure in winter, when I heard below the repeated honking of a cab like a flock of migrating geese out of season. This honking was at the curbside entrance to the first floor of the abandoned warehouse and naturally my first thought was, "Charlie's back in a cab unable to pay the fare and is summoning me down to pay if for him with a blood donation. Or have authorities come to take me back to that island resort in East River?"

Torn between these two speculations, I stand in the plywood enclosure, listening, quivering between apprehension and hope beyond despair, till a human voice calls out my name below, the voice of a female, not Charlie's, but nevertheless I clatter breathlessly down the flight of stairs to the street level, to find in the doorless doorway the Actress Invicta, heroically black-cloaked, with a face out of Greek tragedy, lifted as if for declamation on-stage.

With this powerful vocal instrument of hers, she asks of me, "Is he up there with you and who's it he cut out with, since he is not at Phoebe's or anyplace else I've spent the whole night searching?"

I was too breathless to say more than "Who?"

"My God!"

"I don't know who your God is."

"The Big Lot of my life!"

"Please don't shout so. We are vis-à-vis with equal griev-
ances: this is not a stage confrontation, you know."

"What I want's information, not Cowardly one-liners at
this hour!"

"Yes, night's full of hours, but Charlie is not in residence
and Big Lot's never been on my visiting list since I dropped
out of his."

"Oh? No?"

"Want to come up and see?"

She started to enter but retreated, probably for the first
time in her existence.

Dramatically, she dropped her voice.

"You know that's not funny."

"I didn't mean it to be and I do understand your protective feeling for Lot as well as I don't understand his
exploitive treatment of you."

"Then you don't know about love."

"Let's not argue that point in this icy doorway."

"A woman's love is different."

"Are you going or staying?" shouted the cabman.

"Going, just a moment," she shouted back to him, pro-
jecting her voice again as if to a second balcony of a large
Broadway house.

Her eyes became huge as they faced mine once more.

"I've rarely been through such an awful night in my life."

"Neither have I."

"That thing at Moise's. I was so shaken up by her appearance, I mean her condition and that see-through rag she
was wearing, that I couldn't make out much of her an-

nouncement, but didn't it contain an appeal to reach Tony Smith in South Orange?"

"Yes, it did."

"Well, please let her know I can reach him through Celebrity Service and will start on it today. I know both Jane and Tony, have known them since my Hollywood days with Franz, and I know that they will respond to her appeal, but meanwhile will you please give Moise this twenty?"

"Yes. Of course. I will."

"Thanks. Now tell me, where on earth do you think I can find Lot?"

"You could find him wherever I would find Charlie if I knew where."

"That's a bitch of an answer."

"Ain't it just?"

"You understand, don't you?"

"I don't understand and don't know."

Just at that moment, a cat streaked out of the warehouse with a squealing thing in its jaws.

"My God," she said, "this is worse than the Dakota!"

The scene then became scrambled by a tall and dark human figure crossing the street toward the cab and the cab starting off and the actress crying out, "Lot."

When the scene unscrambled, the actress was confronting the tall figure which she had hysterically mistaken for Lot and was shrilling at him, "Do you suppose I'd be on this corner at this hour without a revolver on me!"

The man crossed away, much smaller.

"Would you like to come in and wait with me till later?"

I don't think she heard me.

She stalked away in her heroic black cloak as if she

had never heard of danger at a wolf's hour in her life, and as I went back up the stairs I said to myself, "Well, now I know that love is demolition."

But having returned to the hooked rectangle, I correct that facile and small definition of the only thing that is larger than life by the following bit of rhetoric.

"Among the things love includes, unlimited as life and perhaps as death, there is demolition of self and possibly also of the object of the love! Which led me back to that long-ago whisper of Moise's, 'It isn't good but it's God.'"

Without at first being aware of what it was in the room that was no longer there, that was very disturbingly missing (and I don't mean Charlie), I sat before BON AMI, pencil clutched, watching, listening, alert as, say, an aged and crippled villager of some distant embattled country would watch and listen skyward at the sound or sight of approaching enemy planes. I don't believe that I knew, at first, whether it was the sound or sight of something that had ceased to be present in the hooked rectangle number one to infinity of my existence. I was, of course, stupefied, much as I was while sitting in tense silence (which was my own only) in a corner of the violent ward on the island in the River East.

(Forgive these scrambled images, my hands shake like my thoughts as I now continue to attempt to write in very small but legible script on laundry cardboard #2.)

What had stopped was that hitherto faithful sound of the one-legged clock which I had removed to the furthest possible corner within the rectangle's confines but which, though muted by that distance, had still been audible to me and so reassuring to me as a familiar presence. Yes. It—it had now stopped dead, and the fact that I had simply not wound it up that night did not improve the omen of its suddenly noticed cessation. I suppose I felt as an old man must feel who has lived his whole life, or the important half of it, beside a mountain cataract, and one day or night, half-emerging from the dream that time has gently drawn him into, notices that the eternity of that waterfall's murmur has been stilled without warning.

Clock-beat, heartbeat: you don't want to hear either, but you always trust their going on with you, for otherwise you'd stop, too.

Stopping, stopping, who wants it, even from an old travesty of a clock or a heart worn out at thirty.

Now there will be no future way of knowing if it is still night or into morning without periodic ventures into the cat-and-rat battleground of the loft outside.

After it did become clear to me that it was the clock's sound which had stopped, I went once again into that no-man's-land and saw through its windows that time was indeed into morning, dimmed by the dust of the windows and by dockside fog. I stood there, paralyzed by bereavement, for time enough to accept a totally new condition of life.

And then I sneezed, once, twice, repeatedly. I touched my forehead and found it burning as his body had burned, and whispered to myself, "I won't survive it."

(I won't read back through this passage for the embarrassing footprints of self-pity, that most despicable emotion of humankind still living, for it would stop me dead on cardboard #2 like the clock.)

Then, then, then.

Behind me I heard sounds, not the clock's, not mine, within the hooked rectangle, and I turned that way and moved toward the narrow opening of the plywooded section that would admit you thinly.

And there was Charlie back from his all-night excursions, not greeting me but looking down at my army-store boots as he unlaced them.

It was I that broke the silence.

"Charlie, I think I'm dead."

"But still at work on BON AMI."

"Naturally, what else?"

"Shit."

"Probably, since I've spent the night alone, obsessed with"

"Huh?"

"A positive frenzy of lascivious"

"Thoughts of me and your spade that cracked through the ice?"

"I have arrived at something."

"Such as?"

"Recognition of you."

"Never now or ever."

"No, I think at last I know you, Charlie."

"Bully for you, old sport. Now why'nt you go out and look at that green light on Daisy's dock and eat your heart out in private?"

"It's the truth, like Scott and Jack Clayton told it."

"Well, go and skate on it, I'm dog tired and I intend to sleep."

"Alone."

"Hope so."

Now he was removing his clothes with the leisure of a

stripteaser, instinctively provocative even now, but the provocation was not of the kind to which he was accustomed when unclothing.

It wasn't loathing or hatred on a conscious level, but it was building to something that could crack thick ice with the ease of a toothpick through a pitted olive.

I looked at him as he slowly stripped himself bare and crawled into bed; then he spoke and what he said was like a quotation from something.

"Infidelities are not confined to the present."

He meant that I had loved the ice skater for those thirteen years until he, Charlie, had come into my life, one week after the ice skater had cracked the goddam ice forever, meaning retired into the silent ice world forever and no more skating on it, through a possibly accidental or deliberate OD on—you name it, I never knew, all that I knew was that he alternated continually between big highs and lows and was constant only to beauty. And I *don't* mean me. . . .

•

"Well, Charlie, tell me about it, what was it and how did it go?"

"Don't start that shit."

"What shit?"

"The questions bit, I don't need it."

"I know you don't need it any more than I do but I suspect that you'd like to tell me something about it."

"I don't much care if I tell you but I will. After the thing at Moise's, Big Lot said that you were going to stay with her and he said, 'Let's drop by the Factory,' and we did and LaLanga was there. All right, he was there, and this thing happened between us. You know, Big Lot and I had run out with the bottle of red Gallo and we drank it on the way to the Factory and I saw LaLanga as a living poem which I know that he is and I also know that what he put in my body was a poem, too!"

"Oh. So."

"Yes."

I knew that I had lost Charlie to the living poems of poets and what remained of what I had thought was a poem between us was now expiring like that warm aromatic bit of a candle last evening at Moise's.

Isn't it always like that, in the world, gay or straight?

My answer to that is yes. It simply takes longer in some cases than others for ice skaters to stop skating on the ice but to enter it for the silence of forever.

"Going out?"

"That's right. Goodbye, Charlie."

"Where you think you're going, man, at this hour?"

"I'm going back to Moise's."

"I don't think you'll get in there."

"What gives you that impression?"

"Refugees from the party say that when the candle burnt out there was a sort of riot. A pregnant girl was trampled kind of bad and somebody hollered police and Moise bolted the door and Big Lot says it'll never be opened again unless the great red-bearded father in South Orange gets the message and breaks down the door."

"Goodbye," I said again. Then with that touch of bitchiness that can never be quite excluded from lovers parting, I said, "Watch out for the sudden subway, that's all, Charlie."

"Huh?"

(Perfunctorily spoken.)

"Goodbye."

"Oh, are you really going back to Moise's?"

"Naturally."

"Why?"

"Okay, I'll tell you. If I got in bed with you I would profane the poem LaLanga and I don't want to do that."

"I wouldn't allow you to."

"No. So. Goodbye."

"You say goodbye instead of good night to me."

"That's right."

"Why?"

I didn't answer that till after I had put on the army coat and muffler which he'd thrown off, and then, as I started toward the door, removing the ice skater's photo from its hook on the dingy wall, I said to Charlie, "I'm going to Moise's and although to go there now is to return there sooner than expected and certainly sooner than I'd be welcome, it would be much more appropriate than—"

I started out the door and Charlie said, "That was an incomplete sentence but what else is life made of?"

"Well, in Ethiopia the nomadic tribes who live by their cattle have lost ninety-eight percent of their cattle in a big drought there and I saw a picture today of vultures sitting on a long line of telegraph poles along the road to the sea, waiting for anything that might come along there."

"Yes, that's life, too," said Charlie, his voice still perfunctory.

Now I had this last door almost closed between us and he said one more thing.

"Skates said she'd killed Moise."

"I hardly think so, Charlie."

But I hesitated a few moments longer at the door.

"What gave Skates that impression?"

"It's been going on a long time," said Charlie with an indifferent yawn, not even turning to give me a glance as I lingered one last moment.

"Yes, I know that the malice of Skates is practically inexhaustible as the lecheries that you mistake for a love life."

"How's that so, lover boy?"

Then he did turn to look at me and I would not have believed it possible that he could look at me in such a different way than I had known, well, either known or imagined, for nearly two years. That was a thing that had to be turned away from and not carried with me from the makeshift partitions of our section of the dockside loft, no, it would not go with me like the photo of the lover I'd removed from the wall.

He seemed to be looking with real contempt at me now, no, it wasn't possible, it wasn't part of the world of reason, and yet there it was, the cold knife of his look hurled at me as I waited.

"You hardly think so, you hardly think anything but that creatures like you and Moise can survive on nothing. Are you a couple of air plants, is this the tropics? Why, Christ, you pitiful son of a bitch, you won't live through the flu at Moise's or on the streets of this city. Moise has packed it with Skates's assistance, she knows it's finished with her, but you, ho, man, you think that old photo of a spade which thank God you're taking out of here with you and your demented pieces of writing will suffice to keep you going, well, man, the truth is nothing to what you're going to face."

"Charlie, the trouble with you is that you mean the truth is nothing."

I came back into the room and kicked the door shut so violently that it fell backward onto the landing.

"Don't you come near me!"

"Oh, I'm never coming closer to you again than I am now, but I want to tell you something. I happen to love LaLanga as a poet but you don't know a poem from ejaculations of sperm in your butt which is not always going to be haunch of venison, baby, nope, you'll discover that being buggered by a poet hasn't injected you with his talent and it never will and that is the truth which is something, not nothing, as in your adolescent opinion, and your opinions will not mature but simply wither on you, and you and Skates may think that you have the power to defoliate the world with your falsities and your venom, but, hell, baby, the world will defoliate you because your eyes, the look in them, is like the hiss of Skates, and you know why she did that to Moise, it was because Tony Smith has lectured on the work of Moise and has no knowledge of Skates and Skates is so invidious by nature and so aware in her bone-dry heart, I mean her hissing center of being, not to be called a heart if you live in the world of reason or beyond it, that she is an imitator of Moise but will never make it and will survive because of her side-line of newspaper illustrations of women's wear at thrift prices, and nothing will advance her in what she fancies is her creative calling, her vocation she has the nerve to call it, not fooling even herself, and as for that hiss at Moise, I can assure you, *cunt divine,* that Moise didn't hear it, she certainly didn't heed it, and I can assure you, too, that the hiss of a snake called Skates has never and could never kill anybody, even if it was heard and heeded."

"Look," said Charlie, "you have kicked down the door which is the only effectual gesture you have made in your life which is finished. Now get through the space where it used to be quick as you can haul your tired ass out of my life to the apparition of Moise, Christ, did any two people belong so much to each other? I belong to LaLanga and tomorrow am posing for Andy and Big Lot says that with you out of my way there is nothing can stop me!"

Of course these words rang like the fire bells and police sirens of hell as I staggered down the steps and out into the almost impenetrable iciness of the street, wondering if Moise had indeed bolted the door quite finally against the world of reason and would not hear or heed my knock and cry for admittance.

But it occurred to me then that I was not a part of the world of reason which she had announced no longer tenable to her, and besides, to wonder if she would hear me and heed me was like wondering if God, as abstraction or persona, had ever existed and I remain incorrigibly a believer.

The ice of the air softened then, and I moved east on Eleventh and crossed to Bleecker, witlessly and serenely, holding the photo snatched from the rectangle's wall like a cross above me.

For of the earth's frozen waters I wanted now only the ditch where a child crouched at dusk to release from his fingers a paper boat, as frail as a May butterfly, and if the ditch water is frozen, apologies to Rimbaud for these recurrent images of ice.

III

However, that haunting last image, somewhat paraphrased in the lifting from Rimbaud's *Bâteau Ivre,* has to be fractured now by the account of an incident, unsuitably raw and vicious as the lash of a bullwhip. I would prefer to omit it, but since it occurred I shall have to include it and accept the shattered mood of what could well have served as the curtain lines to an atmospheric play or to a composition for a well-tempered clavichord.

I don't like theater because I don't like curtains: they always seem contrived and I don't like contrivances. I guess this aversion to completion is another serious flaw in my concept of creative work. When Moise completes a canvas it is truly completed, even to the almost indistinguishable *M* that is her signature and that is worked into the painting as if it were a part of it. She believes in curtains, in completion, but she accomplishes it, this completion, as if it were there, visible to herself only, from the beginning, an instinct of a thing's fullness or perfection which has always eluded me in my course through the Blue Jays of my life.

Well, she's a visionary, she works in a state of trance that cannot be broken without shocking consequence to herself and the strictly ordered anarchy which she lives in. That is the wrong way to put it. It is making out of it something that sounds more like an aphorism than a simple truth. It is a kind of magic to which I'm not initiated, it seems, and when I try to discuss it I resort to wrong words such as "strictly ordered anarchy" which is a phrase that doesn't stand scrutiny. Lance would say "shit." Moise would say nothing but would probably throw something at me. Or would have a spasm, one of those seizures that only come upon her when a trance is disturbed by the intrusion of something or someone that is alien to her "room" and I put the word "room" in quotes because its meaning is larger than room, it is her world and existence.

It was once only Lance and then it became Lance and me who were trusted to watch her at work.

"There is the wooden spoon, dear."

She would point out a rather grimy-looking tongue depressor on a table by her easel with a challenging smile that Lance understood but did not explain to me.

Obviously Moise did not have these attacks when she was working under conditions entirely within her control: I think it's also obvious that she liked the presence of Lance and later of Lance and me when she was at work on a painting even though there was always the possibility that even a very familiar and loved presence might disturb the inwardly strong current of her way through a painting. It was understandable to me as an image. Her work on a canvas had the compulsive flow toward completion that a mountain stream has toward the basin it is drawn into: a cataract that emptied into a state of rest like the seventh day of Genesis, and Lance would say "shit" to that too, and I learned soon not to question or notice the point at which her initial *M* was painted onto the lower right-hand corner of a canvas in such a way that it seemed a part of it from the beginning.

I may return to this nearly inscrutable history of Moise at work later, but I have mentioned an incident that took place as I made my crazy way from West Eleventh to Bleecker.

To go directly into an account of this brutal incident would still be too abrupt. I feel that I have not yet told you enough about the room of Moise as it was when Lance and I were admitted there every night when he was not on tour with his ice show.

Almost since I first came to know Moise I've kept a Blue Jay notebook in her Bleecker Street room, usually two of them, and the contents of these Blue Jays are devoted almost entirely to the spoken reveries that she's inclined to go into while holding a brush or paint-smudged finger before a canvas. I don't think she knows she is talking since she always appears quite startled when these reveries are interrupted by my voice or much more rarely by Lance's when Lance was still with me.

In those old days Lance was far more discreet than I when she started talking while painting. He would usually be as quiet as possible, removing his shoes so that his steps on the creaky floor would be less apt to disturb her and when I would interject a comment or question he would most likely place a hand over my mouth with a warning gesture toward Moise.

"*What, what, what?*" she would cry with a look of broken enchantment.

"Nothing, honey, *rien de tout, ma chère!*" Lance would whisper and she would drift into her reveries and her hesitations of finger or brush before the "The Mystery" which was her name for each unfinished painting.

I was thinking of these Blue Jays I kept at Moise's as I approached her "atelier" on Bleecker through the mist of the winter morning when the headlights of a prowl car cut through it and stopped just behind me on the street.

Needless to say I have wasted no affection on police cars, especially when I'm alone on the streets of that section at such a desolate hour.

I pretended to ignore the car slowing down close behind me till a menacingly macho voice bawled out, "Hey there, drop what you're holding, turn to the wall and put your hands against it."

"Do you mean me?"

"I said drop what you're holding and"

"It's a framed photo with glass."

I didn't drop it, of course, but lowered it slowly from its position over my head. With the quick and incongruous images of fever shuttling through my brain, I recognized the gesture of lowering Lance's photo slowly from over my head to directly before my face as that of a priest handling a chalice at Mass and this image startled from me something between a laugh and a gasp. I didn't hear the car door open or slam shut or the heavy officer's steps but

I gasped again, this time without a laugh, as the photo was snatched from my hand.

"It's a naykid man's pitcher."

"It isn't a naked man's picture, it's a photograph of an ice-skating star in tights."

"Another pervert. Git him aginst that wall."

I was wheeled roughly about to face the corner building and shoved against it and hands began to frisk me. My fever must have exaggerated their size and brutality. I hate to admit it, but the mauling was almost pleasurable, I think it must have reminded me somewhat of Lance's occasionally violent approach to lovemaking when I was sitting up with a Blue Jay too long to suit him.

"What's all these papers on yuh?"

"Literary works I'm moving to"

"You're moving to the car."

Then I felt something hard and cold clamped about my ankles, pulling them together.

Handcuffs, on my ankles, and told to move?

"How and where?"

"You're goin' to the station."

"Grand Central or Pennsylvania?" I shouted with a burst of hysteria.

"Nobody likes a smart ass unless he fucks it."

He wheeled me from the building and sprawled me into the gutter with a shove.

"Christ, you've broke my wrists."

"I'll break ev'ry goddam bone in your cock-suckin' body if you don't hop like a toad, tha's right, hop or crawl it and make it quick."

Looking up at his face I saw it was hardly visible through

the winter daybreak fog and I trusted that my face was equally indefinite to him.

"I think you should know you're molesting a minor without offense."

It didn't make much sense and the result was a vicious kick in the butt.

I know it's incredible but it is possible to live half your life in this city and never encounter an incident of this nature without any provocation but odd behavior in public.

"I am not going to hop and I am not going to crawl and if you were on the job, the Actress Invicta wouldn't have had to scare a mugger away from West Eleventh."

"Kick him in," said the officer in the car.

The kick was repeated, harder.

"Heh heh heh."

It was a guttural New York red-neck laugh that reminded me of all the unidentified bodies, young and old, some of them stripped and mutilated, discovered in empty lots and trash bins or dropped off bridges in the five furious boroughs of the city.

"Christ, oh, Christ," I said, dropping flat onto the street.

At this moment, precisely, a tall, thin figure emerged from the Bleecker Street mist, and it was Moise, still in her transparent garment.

"What are you savages doing to my brother?" she demanded with a vocal power I didn't know she possessed.

The other officer now hopped out of the prowl car and went up to her apparitional figure.

"What are you?"

"I am still who, not what. And you are a pair of apes in public service and I am not just a member of the public but one with the highest connections."

A window lighted across the street; an old woman's face peered out.

"Lady, lady," I called but her response was to draw her head back in the window and switch the light off.

The officers glanced at each other. One nodded, the other shook his head.

The one who had nodded now spoke in a mock-polite voice.

"How would you and your brother like a little ride around the neighborhood, Miss?"

"Moise, a witness looked out a window," I gasped.

"Unnecessary, not at all necessary," said Moise, "I phoned headquarters before I came outside."

The cops muttered together, then one said aloud, "Le's quit foolin' with this coupla nuts."

My ankles were unshackled by one while the other attempted to give Moise a libidinous feel.

I heard a loud slap.

"Resisting. Indecent."

"Shit, it's morning, le's go."

Car door slam, motor starting.

We were alone on the corner.

"Jesus God."

"Who?"

"I've lost Lance's picture."

"There are duplicates of it."

She had gathered up the literary properties which the officers had scattered on the street.

"How did you know this was going on, Moise?"

"Mystery but simple."

(Perhaps she'll explain it later.)

IV

WHEN A PLACE contains no clock or watch, that circumstance does not dismiss my concern with the passage of time: it is more inclined to accentuate it. The winter light admitted by the large window in the back wall is the only timekeeper here, and I find myself, today at Moise's, glancing again and again that way to surmise what hour it is, but the window is frosted over and its function as timekeeper is very far from precise. Why it is frosted over I don't know, since there's no heat at Moise's except that of my fever and my anxiety and her quietly living presence.

For I am anxious despite Moise's Buddhistic calm. I am not reconciled to drifting out of existence even with her. I try to make conversation between us but she is either inaudible in her replies or monosyllabic. I know she prefers my presence to being completely alone in her retirement from the world of reason (or unreason), but she is keeping her counsel, not in a way that is catatonic, but in a way that is more like waiting for a verdict of *yes* or *no* and not wanting to be distracted from this passive waiting by my efforts to engage her in talk. She is sitting on the edge of her bed as a female deity might and she hasn't glanced once at the large frosted window, seeming not to share my concern with time-passage at all.

Lance would have advised me to keep my mouth shut, but since Lance is long gone from this room and all others of which I know, his admonitions are also permanently absent and I persist in trying to entice Moise out of her chilling silence.

"Moise?"

"Yes? Now what?"

"Will you please talk to me, we are sitting here like strangers in the waiting room of a station."

"Doesn't everybody do that who sits anywhere with someone?"

"No. It was never like that when Lance"

"When Lance, when Lance, it's like the flower of knighthood, that far away from our present existence."

"I know, but I did hope that when you let me back in the room there'd be a little comforting communication between us, if only by signs or glances, but you sit there completely sunk into your thoughts, you're remote as the Himalayas to a traveler without passport or means of passage."

"Well, I will break my silence to tell you this. There's always been something a little marked-down, a little depreciated about your character since Lance's departure and the advent of your catamite on the prowl. I must tell you that you writers, you people of the literary persuasion, you substitute words and phrases, slogans, shibboleths and so forth for the simplicities of true feeling. Put a few words in what you think is a clever arrangement, and you feel absolved of all authentic emotion."

(It had struck me till this outburst that Moise in her improvised see-through garment was almost without bodily sensation or mental animation, that she was suspended in both: she breathed without sound and hardly perceptible motion of her chest, and if her eyelids flickered, they did it in a way that escaped observation. Now I knew that she was in a turmoil of feeling that made my own seem relatively serene.)

"This doesn't seem like you at all."

Her response was a four-letter vulgarism which she had never used before, at least not in my presence. Vulgarisms of word or deed did not seem in her province, they seemed to belong outside the door on Bleecker, despite the confessions made the evening before of "unnatural relations" with the patron "eighty-seven at Bellevue."

"*Scriveners fuck off.*"

"Why?"

"When have you ever gotten out of your skins, your crocodile hides, to exhibit anything but yourselves and your blah-blah cleverisms? You can't see life through your lives which stink to the devil's nostrils. Yes, put that down in your Blue Jay."

"Moise, I don't recognize you."

"You thought I was complicated, not a simple barbarian. And you say I am thinking but I am not thinking at all. Thinking involves cogitation like wrestling mentally with specific problems which I am not doing. What I'm doing's reflecting, and reflecting's knowing of things which are not problems since they have no solution, none whatsoever,

which are simply fixed conditions that only time and
mortality can affect, I mean in a terminal fashion, and
don't use the word 'semantics,' don't throw that fucking
word at me or I will know that you're a familiar of that
horrible red-bearded professor at NYU that even Mary
McCarthy's dropped like a sizzling hot rock."

"Still I would like to know the subject of your reflections."

"All right, you shall and I think you'll be sorry. I was reflecting upon the fact that there is such a profusion of
crones in this city."

Well.

My natural cunning advised me to profess ignorance of
the word "crones," and as for her reflection upon their
profusion in the city, this was indeed peculiar, for though
Moise has about her a timeless quality, she is certainly not
old.

"What is a crone, Moise?"

"Look it up in a dictionary," she replied sharply.

"All right, where's the dictionary?"

"If there is a dictionary it will be in"

She pointed to a cabinet built into the opposite wall.
It contained a curious mélange of "found objects" and so
forth, the most remarkable of which was a copy of *Who's
Who* for 1952.

"Why do you keep a copy of *Who's Who* for 1952?" I
asked her.

"Because in 1952 a society lady I met by accident on
upper Park took up my acquaintance, wanted me for a
model, she was an amateur painter of portraits, a wretched
old thing of no talent but much academic training and
afflicted with a malignancy that her doctors fooled her
about, declared her health to be perfect except for ad-

hesions from her last operation. Well, that's neither here nor there. She took me under the wing of her enormous wealth for some weeks, which is a pertinent detail, and one day she said, 'I want to give you a party, sort of a debut, here, look in this book and give me the names of the guests you want invited from it.' She gave me that *Who's Who* for 1952. Well. It so happened that I did have a relative named Coffin who was in the book, but this relative was afflicted with chronic melancholia, she had purchased two hundred thousand dollars' worth of Belgian lace when a dreadful attack of the melancholia came on her and she left the lace exposed, nobody dared to touch it except an army of moths which destroyed it almost completely. Well. I called this relative Coffin and she appeared to be on the upswing of her cycle and she actually accepted the invitation to the debut party. I then took the liberty of inviting my close friends not listed in *Who's Who* but on the subversive lists and welfare rolls. Well. The relative Coffin never recovered from it and neither did the Park Avenue lady, summoned a doctor far too late for medical intervention and died in the elevator from her two-story penthouse. The 1952 *Who's Who* I have kept as a memento of her short-lived patronage, love. Now what have you picked up?"

"Moise, I've discovered a candle and a book of matches."

"Oh, my God, for his sake. Is it one of my thick, aromatic candles?"

"Yes, identical to last evening's and is intact."

I placed the candle on the table, replaced *Who's Who* in the cabinet, and returned to sit by Moise. She drew a long breath and then said, "Christ on a crossbeam, lofted, you said 'What is a crone' as if you'd never noticed them crouching on doorsteps in all weather or leaning out of windows to suck in breath or, in the midtown section, you must have passed through it sometime, they creep about the streets where they congregate singly."

" 'Congregate singly' is a"

"Yes, but they do, it's the truth, there's no contradiction about it. The midtown section is infested with crones and the *wanderings* of them, my God."

"So, crones . . ."

I believe that I was justifiably disappointed in Moise at this moment, for here I had been crouching like a priest in the shrine of a sibyl, Blue Jay and pencil in cold-stiffened fingers, trusting her to emerge from her silent revery with speech of a pure and elevating nature, oracular utterances that contained the quality of which the poet Keats must have been dreaming when he referred to "huge, cloudy symbols of a high romance," and now that I had provoked her to speech, she had spoken of nothing more inspired or inspiring than what I've now transcribed, faithfully as I could, in my last notebook. She had sat there looking like Garbo as Karenina or Camille: then had produced a verbal accompaniment to that image as incongruous as a bathetic score by Max Steiner. I know, of course, that a terminal situation frequently draws the victim in a descent to, not a rise to, new levels of concern. I also know that the true nature of a person's concerns in extreme circumstances may be obscured by sayings that are inappropriate if not altogether irrelevant to the awesome finality of a situation such as seemed to enclose Moise in her world retired from reason.

" 'Ah, Harry, thou hast robbed me of my youth,' " I quoted from the bard.

Her reply was a scatological expletive which I prefer to

delete and a slight but ferocious shrug of her shoulders and a hitch away from me on the bed.

"You wanted me to talk and now I'm talking and there's nothing funny about it, I can assure you that I am as humorless as the invincible living actress or the great narcissan of diarists, Anima Nimes."

"Moise, have you caught the fever that I caught from Charlie?"

"I am *immune*," she shouted, yes, she literally shouted, "to fevers contracted from catamites on the prowl."

"But you are talking with the extravagance of fever."

"I believe I am shouting."

"Yes, you are crying out like a heretic put to the rack who is in such pain that she"

"Denies, confesses, *même chose*."

"Perhaps you are worried about the problem of future prospects."

"Not in the least since my time has already broken the tape of its distance. You know that my life-style has dropped far below the level of subsistence which it barely approached in the past except for the month I modeled and made a debut for poor Miss *Who's Who* on Park. I suppose that Scott Fitzgerald would have observed a great mystic difference between a very rich crone and a destitute crone, but when I remember that old Park Avenue lady, besieged by relatives gasping for her demise, spending her time either painting without vision or filling enormous scrapbooks with clippings about her idol Senator Joseph McCarthy and his crusade against radical infiltration and going to The Colony for lunch which she couldn't digest, which she'd vomit after two bites despite its incomparable quality in '52. No, crones are crones and wealth or destitution makes no difference in their desperation, except that maybe the ones that sit on winter doorsteps with dirty wrappings about their legs are distracted by physical sensation in a more fortunate way. But in the midtown section where I lived before Bleecker, I tell you there was a real profusion of crones and they crept about the streets like snails, all about the same height and color, for camouflage purposes, I guess, and all with one hand trailing the walls and the other hand clutching a cane or a stick and they never have pocketbooks with them, sometimes they manage to clutch a brown paper bag filled with refuse they've gathered in alleys, they clutch it under the arm that has the hand with the cane, and, oh, they're gray, they're past gray, clothes, faces and hands, all that camouflage gray for protection from death. Instinct takes them outdoors and cunning brings them back in and they dwindle away like the ranks of veterans of old wars in Memorial Day parades. But there are always replacements. Always new crones. They never look at you since they don't want to be noticed and they don't carry pocketbooks because they can't cry out or lift a hand in defense if the pocketbooks should be snatched."

A pause: then:

"I have recently learned that my mother has turned into a crone."

Well, now I understood why she had embarked on the subject.

"How did this information come to you, Moise?"

"The information came to me through a message slipped under my door. It was a long letter from an old friend of mine who informs me that my mother has not only turned to a crone but to a scavenger crone. She jiggles public phones for silver to eat at a cheap diner in the midtown section. This friend reproaches me for it. She says that my mother comes out of her cold furnished room in the late afternoon with one hand trailing the walls and the other clutching a cane. She refuses to look into this friend's eyes or respond to her greetings. She makes a turn of five or six blocks in the midtown section and sneaks into public phone booths and jiggles the hooks for small change to eat at a greasy-spoon diner that's worse than an Automat in SoHo and this old friend who claims that she pays Mother's room-rent reproaches me severely for abandoning my mother to these circumstances. As if I could do otherwise in my own situation on Bleecker. This friend suggests that I should bring her to Bleecker or move back to midtown and provide for her there. Provide for her how? By what means? Of course it can't be considered. It's a terminal thing, nothing at all to be done, she'd hardly know me, and how could I bear to know her in this state of a scavenger which she's fallen into? It isn't as if"

"What?"

"She could ever stand me or I could ever stand her. When I took up painting she said I was destined for prostitution or lunacy or both and she threw a suitcase at me and told me to hit the streets. And that's how I moved to Bleecker."

Her gray eyes darkened as if reflecting the nightfall and she lapsed into silence again, for which I was almost grateful. I had never known her to speak in so bitter a fashion upon a subject which, if not tragic, surely contained a considerable pathos, and of her own mother, whether loved or regretted. As recently as the evening before I would have been young enough to be moved to tears but now my youth and the sentiments of it were passed, in fact

I was happy that the room contained no mirror, for if I'd looked in it, it might have reflected a face a hundred years older, eligible for casting as the Dalai Lama or Dorian Gray at the end of his transference from portrait to self-ravaged flesh.

I suppose in some unacknowledged corner of my heart I still possessed the typical Southern attitude toward mothers, something between the maudlin and the unfathomably awful, but certainly never detached, the umbilical cord not merely remaining unsevered but drawn even tighter through time, and the dispassionate, no, that isn't the word, what I mean is the fierce reportage quality of Moise's chronicle of her mother's decline, reminding me of Capote's *In Cold Blood,* made me feel that I was not with Moise as I had known her before.

The gentleness had gone from her as scent from a dried flower and even her classic beauty in the see-through garment had a suspicion of artifice about it.

She didn't appear to notice my shocked reaction but when she resumed her speech it was in a much softer tone.

"You see, I am now convinced that Moppet is dead."

"Moppet is?"

"No, no, Moppet *was.*"

"But isn't 'moppet' the Hollywood term for a child on the screen?"

"Yes, in the cases of Temple and O'Brien, but in the case of this Moppet, it wasn't a child star but a canine crone, a dog which was the only remaining bond between my mother and me."

"You've never mentioned this dog Moppet before."

"I have mentioned her now that I know she's no longer, and even before I left the apartment in the midtown section, Moppet had turned to a crone and to a scavenger crone. She had a voracious appetite and you couldn't get her past a garbage pail on the street, she was well-fed at home but still was unnaturally hungry and when taken out for a walk she would forget to pee, she was so mad for the garbage pails on the street, you could hardly drag her past them, she acquired a preternatural strength when you tried to make her move past a garbage pail and, oh, my God, the way that she would look at you with her great brown eyes through her mop of dirty gray hair, I'm sorry, don't let me cry, but it was so completely heartbreaking, the huge appetite of this little dog no bigger than a magnified insect. And I would so want to let her spend an hour at each garbage pail, but, you see, her digestion was shot. I took her to a vet's and he told me that she was probably so hungry because her digestive system was no longer able to absorb nourishment, love. And if I am crying, that is why I am crying, because Moppet is gone and Mother"

She stopped or became inaudible.

"I understand now, Moise. You are distressed that your mother has assumed the character of Moppet."

"Yes, precisely, how dare she?"

"You're being a little unreasonable, Moise."

"Completely and why not, *chez moi* and *entre nous?*"

"It must have been more than fifteen years since you left the midtown section, and is it true that you left because your mother threw a piece of luggage at you?"

"Christ," said Moise, "what are you talking about, my mother threw a piece of luggage at me? That's the last thing on earth she would have had sense enough to think of doing, my dear. On the contrary, she tried to block the door when I informed her that I was leaving for good. She threw herself against the door with her arms spread out like Jesus on a cross but I was possessed with a superhuman power and I flung the door open and she fell to the floor and Moppet tried to follow me into the street."

Again her voice became inaudible. I was afraid to look at her, it was so icy cold in the room.

At last I took hold of her hand.

"There is a parallel to my departure from Thelma, you know, and to my own flight from my mother on West Eleventh when she fell on the street and was arrested as drunk."

"Exactly, a parallel, yes, and that is why you are here and I am here in this icy room together. We are a pair of monsters by the same edict of law. There is a difference, though. You have alternatives to it, one of which you'll accept. I mean you won't stay here long "

"Do you mean you plan to evict me?"

"No, heavens, no. Evict you I would never. However I do know your nature. You are influenced by Mars with Venus rising. All signs portend that you will voluntarily move back into the world outside."

"Moise, that is your suggestion to me but not my impulse, you know."

"Possibly not at this moment but other moments will come. And so will another person. Your nature is"

"What?"

"Evanescent, you're evanescent by nature. Infinitely variable as the snake of the Nile, my child."

(I then took up a Blue Jay and began writing these things down. And a number of things that preceded. I don't know how long it took me but when I'd stopped writing the atmosphere of the room was colder and darker. You know, it is not quite clear to me how much of this story is written in Blue Jays, how much on laundry cardboards and how much on rejection slips and the envelopes they came in, but a great deal has certainly been written, so much that I hardly dare to believe that it can ever be assembled into anything like what could be described as even an ordered anarchy, that detestable phrase which I can't seem to avoid.)

Moise is now talking again.

"I suppose I ought to get an animal as a companion very soon now."

"Oh?"

"Yes, one needs some companionship in the end."

"You mean that I won't do?"

"Temporarily only. Don't make me keep repeating my totally accurate analysis of your nature."

In her voice there was a shrillness, almost a shrewishness, that reminded me of how little we can depend on the generally accepted idea that people in the same boat are good boat partners. Or that sharing the bread of desperation, succumbing to the same terminal illness in the company of each other, is bound to provide some comfort. Or was she

I started to say "acting again" but had she ever deliberately put on a performance of anything but Moise which was not a performance since it was being entirely herself. No need for a question mark there.

"Nothing in the world's that totally accurate, Mo."

"How dare you contract my name to Mo. What are you up to, you meretricious little—*faugh!*"

Yes, she did say "faugh," that much outdated utterance of disgust, so unsuitable to her vocabulary, Moise being, in her way, such a very "now" person. And the way she said it has compelled me to use the despised mark of punctuation which I trust hasn't appeared in this chronicle up till now, meaning then.

"Nothing's totally accurate in your world but mine is now more simplistic. Simplistic to the ultimate degree of — Oh, I didn't tell you that my reproachful friend enclosed a snapshot she'd taken of my mother emerging from her midtown quarters to make her telephone rounds without little Moppet. Here it is, look at it and inwardly digest it if you can, I couldn't. She looks like a mummy just unveiled from a sarcophagus, and in her youth"

I looked at the snapshot and couldn't imagine the youth of Moise's mother.

"In her youth my mother had great beauty, or the illusion which is superior to it. She had hopes, once, when young, of a career on the stage, but hopes go astray like plans of, and so forth."

"Did she ever make an appearance on the stage?"

"Oh, that she did, as sure as the Actress Invicta has appeared on stage as regularly as a comet which astronomers know will reappear in the sky at intervals almost as predictable as if the sky is just a big timepiece. Which maybe it is. Isn't that a shuddering thought?"

"Yes, Moise, the sky, when I looked at it last night from the roof of the warehouse, did give me violent shivers. It was the opposite of a companion."

She apparently only picked up the word "companion."

"I'm glad you agree I should have an animal as a companion, but it has to be resourceful. It will have to scavenge because I can't provide for a living soul in the world and anmials have souls."

"How about a cat?"

"What about a cat?"

"I've discovered the warehouse is full of cats and probably also kittens as well as rats. I can go back there tonight and catch you a whole bagful of kittens and you can make a selection and I will return the others unless you want the whole lot."

"One will suffice," said Moise, "but pick it out carefully for me."

"Well, I can pick it out for size and color but I'm not sure I can tell if it is resourceful or not."

"It has to have the capacity to scavenge."

"I think that capacity is born and bred into the bones of most cats."

"Well, now, let's see, it is late January and if you brought me a kitten, it would be influenced by the"

Abruptly she started to move in a spastic fashion and I snatched up the tongue depressor, thinking that she was going into a seizure.

"Oh, for God's sake, no," she cried out when I pressed the wooden spoon against her mouth. "I am not having a fit, you can see I'm not working since I have nothing to work with. It is just so goddam frozen-over as Greenland's mountains in this world without reason."

"I'm sure it's going to get warmer before it gets colder."

"Because it couldn't get colder."

"No, because you will have a warm cat-companion from the warehouse."

"So you say and I'm supposed to believe you."

"I've never lied to you, Moise."

"Everyone always lies to the dying," she whispered.

"The living, perhaps, are inclined to lie to the dying but the dying don't lie to the dying."

"Try to make some sense," she said, "we must try to make some sense."

Moise then lifted a long, fragile hand to my face.

"Love, your chin is bristly, you need a shave, and you mustn't neglect your appearance even here."

"I came without a razor."

"I once had a razor to shave my pubic hair," she remarked dreamily. "You know, I had a certain vanity about my vaginal entrance and I used to keep it hairless as a child's. I've never been fucked, you know, except in the mouth, not due to aversion to the male organ nor puritanical scruples but because I have a militant attitude about the greatest world problem outside of my room, which is an excess of people, population increasing two million a year in this country alone, and probably billions elsewhere."

"I've always admired it."

"The excess of people?"

"No, no, I meant your vaginal orifice, Moise!"

"Oh, but the razor rusted. I don't shave my pubic hair anymore."

"But the pubic hair is so light and downy that your un-violated entrance is quite visible when you don't cross your legs."

"So much for the lips of my vagina," she said, "but I can't accept the image of you with a beard."

"Neither can I but I made a hasty departure without"

"Without living equipment except yourself, and I would say you are much better off without it."

"But it was so warm with its fever in bed. I have no

bitterness toward it, although I know that second love of my life was mostly a creature of self-induced delusion."

She sighed.

"I have little time for friends in my life now, and less for acquaintances, and for enemies, none at all."

(If I'm kept on here, along with the warehouse cat, and it continues this way for a month or so, I wonder if I won't start writing down "quoth Moise" instead of "Moise says." I have a feeling that as her drift toward terminal magic goes on she will start "quothing" instead of speaking, like that raven of Poe's: I can't recall another poet who employed the word "quoth" instead of "said," and I found myself, at this point, drifting into vagrant thoughts about Poe, as read and written about. I remembered that he's reputed to have had no love in his life except for his sister and fantasies such as Lenore and Annabel Lee and Helen in a niche who sailed a thousand ships and probably never shit. And I remember he died on election day in Baltimore, or collapsed on that day, and has ascended to quoth beyond his mortal sorrows and immortal works unquoth. And then my thoughts wander toward the good gray poet Whitman who was probably scared but who dared to celebrate our love and live oaks growing in Louisiana, where he claimed to have had a woman and illegitimate offspring, but scholars have never been able to substantiate any truth in either, and so he is stuck with that horse-car conductor in Washington and the beautiful wounded youths he nursed and comforted in Civil War hospitals. And his *Calamus* poems that shocked the delicate Southerner Lanier into describing Whitman's poetry as a "barbaric yelp above the rooftops of the world," and why not yelp barbarously over the rooftops of this world instead of playing a flute in Philadelphia,

Mister Sidney Lanier? I love you, too: the Marshes of Glynn are exactly as you described them and you wrote a very beautiful line about the latitude of the horizon being so like the tolerance of good men.)

She is speaking again about the cat-companion.

"And the advantage of a warehouse cat is that when it's hungry, it will not look to me for"

"Sustenance, no, it wouldn't."

"Unless, very large and demented by hunger, it looked at my bare feet and arms as edible objects."

I laughed as I thought there was intentional humor in this macabre thought. Moise has always claimed to lack humor, but I've not believed that she lacked this quality which, *without* which, she could not have survived in her "room."

"Moise, you said let's make sense, so let's do make it."

"Sense is exactly what I'm trying to make. I've heard of or read of recluse persons confined with pets who devoured the recluse when the recluse no longer provided for them with anything but his own flesh, living or dead. That end to my existence would be such a scandal that it would obliterate all memory of my work. And so I want you to promise me that when this promised cat-companion has come to stay here, if it has no better sense, you'll drop in now and then, after you have discovered your third love, and that you'll remind me at a suitable point to find a new home for the cat, no, I couldn't find one, you'd have to take it home with your new love."

"At what point would that supposition?"

"When you visit me for the last time and find me incapable of giving it adequate care."

"Yes, I will, I promise."

There was a motionless but restive feeling between us now. We were talking to be talking about something, a giddy sort of talk that people streak into when any discussion must serve to ward off desperation a short while longer.

But that while had run its course now. We'd fallen silent except for chattering teeth, and stayed in that silence until I noticed that the candle placed on the pale blue saucer had not been lighted and said, "Moise, the candle, you didn't light it."

"Oh, merciful savior, no, I'm sorry, child, I'll light it."

Both of us breathed long relieved sighs as she lighted the aromatic candle in the saucer, and the miracle of its glow and the tender emanation of its scent gave us both, I believe, the sense of receiving the sacrament from a saintly old priest.

Under its spell we were as if hypnotized for a while. When she spoke again it was about a piece of hotel stationery that she had picked up among the literary properties on the street.

"This isn't your handwriting."

I took it from her hand and saw that it bore the name of an uptown hotel and then I knew it was the piece of hotel stationery that the derelict playwright began to write on last night when I left him alone for my ascent to the roof.

Beneath the hotel's name and cabalistic insignia there were five stanzas of rhymed verse which would have been illegible if not written in such large capital letters. The poem was titled CYCLOPS EYE and was signed by the derelict playwright with yesterday's date beneath the signature.

"Copy it in your Blue Jay," said Moise.

Since I was no more favorably impressed by the poem than I had been by its author, I was reluctant to have it occupy space in my last Blue Jay, but Moise had not spoken a request but a command.

Being her guest, an inmate of her world, I felt that I must comply and so I copied it out in small but legible script in the notebook: here it is where it doesn't belong at all, in my opinion.

> I have a vast traumatic eye
> set in my forehead center
> that tortures to its own design
> all images that enter.
>
> Conceiving menace in the green
> beneficence of warmth and light
> it cries alarm into the heart
> and moves the hand to strike.
>
> By fall of night all who were near
> are put to flight or slain:
> the eye, dilated still with fear,
> commands an empty plain.
>
> Then slowly as the golden horns
> sound further in dispersion,
> inward does the Cyclops eye
> revolve on dull aversion,
>
> Inward where the heart stripped bare
> of enemy and lover
> returns a burning, foxlike stare
> till darkness films it over.

"Well?" Moise asked, apparently wanting my opinion of it.

"I don't see the flush of immortality on this verse," I said with a shrug.

"Be that as it may, who is he?"

"A stranger, an intruder, who was with me a while last night."

"Tell me more about him."

"There's nothing more worth telling except that he tried to induce me to set out with him on foreign travels."

"Which invitation you thought you declined but which you really accepted."

"That makes no sense since I not only declined but left him alone at BON AMI where he wrote out this verse."

"Your indifference is surprising since the man is yourself grown old!"

"Oh, make sense, Moise."

"What the fuck do you think I've been making, since I have confessed to you things that make the most terrible sense imaginable in this world since you returned to it."

"And I've recorded it faithfully in the—my last Blue Jay."

"Sometimes you try me past endurance with your pencil and notebook. I am a private person. You wouldn't let me be still. You insisted I talk, and I did, to satisfy you. And do you think it's been easy for me to speak of my mother and the late Moppet as scavenger crones? Did you think I wished it recorded, God knows with what distortion, and what vulgarity, for submission to those indifferent or malignant—no, you see, you've worked me into a frenzy when I needed to be preparing quietly for—"

"Moise, don't say what for."

"For posterity in your Blue Jay, is that what you fondly imagined?"

She sprang up, trembling, and cried out, "Scriveners fuck off. The whole pack of you are abominations and monsters of ego with a single exception."

She didn't name the exception but I suppose it was the

writer Jane Bowles, married to one named Paul, for the collected works of Miss Bowles are the only piece of fiction that she keeps in the built-in cabinet for her found objects and so forth.

"Collected and so she died to satisfy the collectors, not knowing, not suspecting that in her anguish she had torn truth from the world."

She fell back onto the bed but not into silence, as I would now have preferred.

"And you," she went on, "about this poet you encountered last night."

"He was more of a has-been playwright attempting a comeback at the Truck and Warehouse."

"Avoid him, he's not for you. His loneliness makes him a monster that would destroy you as surely as your indifference would destroy him."

"Obviously I'm not pursuing him like a coon-dog chasing down the coonskins that this old derelict was wrapped in."

"Yes, suitably clothed in the pelts of beasts on the run. There's something about the description that makes me think I might know him."

"He said he had been here once and he inquired of your health."

"Better than his, both in body and mind, that little I can assure him. He excels only in recognition of himself as demonstrated in this otherwise mediocre piece of verse, written in the future handwriting of you."

At this point she crouched against the wall as if for protection and growled like a beast that is ambushed by a pack of hunters.

"Monsters of loneliness receive and offer no mercy. They go in terrible ways, like heretics of the Spanish Inquisition, and take with them whoever they've caught hold of. They are not saints but only saints can endure them. You say he proposed something to you?"

"Yes, he proposed foreign travel with him twice and was twice rejected."

"You've had a narrow escape. What could be worse than living with your future?"

"I am not in the theater, Moise, I'm sure you know that."

"I would say you are hell-bent in that direction, God help you, love. What has happened to his former companions?"

Then I told her about the lady who grinned like a pirate but was a great lady and that she had now succumbed to cirrhosis and emphysema with complications.

"If you've put that in a Blue Jay, scratch it out. The monster has confessed murder along with love, tear it or scratch it out quickly, such things should not be recorded, especially when they exist in your own future."

"Oh, Moise, when I came here I expected you to say such wise and beautiful things but instead you are filling my last Blue Jay with delirium and folly."

"You asked me to speak, I am speaking, and if it's not what you wanted, fuck what you wanted, all I can give you is temporary refuge from the world of reason to which you'll return with your love number three, whose footsteps I almost hear approaching at this moment."

Her silence shuddered the room of her world for a moment.

"Well?"

I retreated from the challenge in that word to the frost-sheathed window, now delicately prismatic with the candle's glow. It usually has a pacifying effect, the light of a candle, it is a good light to restore things shattered such as silence when ugly things have been spoken, it's a beautiful light by which to make love till you blow it out for sleep.

I would like to have retreated further into the magic world of candlelight refracted by glass between it and deepening winter dusk: a good light to die by.

But Moise repeated the challenge of "*Well?*"

I turned from the window as if forcibly turned. I saw that her head also turned on her long, ageless throat. Her pallor was gone, her eyes were incandescent. I knew that now she was going to speak in that tongue of angels, that glorious, heightened speech for which the Blue Jay is kept here.

"Here!" She hurled the notebook at me, then pencil, and I caught them both as skillfully as an infielder for the Mets: fortunate, since she had risen and stalked to the center of the room as if to a podium with banners behind it.

"Diminished space with increase of occupants! Incontinent spawning of more and more bellies to feed with continually less, shrinkage of rivers and seas, polluted, sea ferns, amoebic life dying, the huge submarine disaster of oxygen-maker the plankton perishing in fouled oceans. And hands of infants suckling will turn to claws at the dry breasts of their mothers, no cross on the door to spare from death by famine. And still the great churches called faiths approve no limit of increase, twist the cross to a cabalistic emblem like the swastika, east, west, in all lands. Nothing is sanctioned but the *sanctity* of the mercifully unborn to enter the world of reason where to live is to clutch and claw for a while and to die with hands empty as hearts.

Oh, withering world, I cannot push thee far enough away from me!"

(She changed her position slightly, the movement stylized as a gesture of Martha Graham. Her right hand touched her groin which had rejected its life-bearing power, a thing she condemned as malign, and so had a flower's first beauty: and with the other hand she made a delicate motion like that of a juggler in space, a gesture of perilous balance without a sense of peril.)

"I know that a few days ago a beautiful blond acrobat executed a dance step on a wire which he'd illegally stretched between the two tallest buildings of the Borough Manhattan, performed a metaphor there when he danced his defiance of death, gracefully, as if to praise it, between those two tallest towers called the Trade Mart Towers, or World Trade something, over the death of the furious borough where to breathe is to wither and blacken the lungs slowly. Oh, he was acclaimed for it, but with no understanding of what it expressed which is *this*."

(Balancing hand now joining the other to cup her vaginal lips.)

"To give death a dare is better than to fertilize the seeds of the famished future's dry-sucking billions. And meanwhile, isn't it true that an international peace corps translates between warring nations and races nothing but what but nothing, while the big mouths blah-blah, this or that blah-blah, written for them to read, memorial pens distributed whenever the blah-blah is signed, oh, everything's said and is signed but a covenant for the only possible things, sucking the seed off or licensing the anus as preferable entrance, with sometimes, of course, a bit of—"

(She turned to her bed, speech over, with an exhausted

smile, that of a devout believer, dying, when the sacrament's done.)

"—a bit of—petroleum—jelly. . . ."

She sat down on the bed.

"Have I been speaking?"

"Yes, quite a lot, Moise."

"What did I say, child?"

"I can't tell you now but I will play it back later from the Blue Jay."

"There's something a little meretricious about you, isn't there, dear?"

(This time she said it no more unkindly than you'd remark to a friend that he seemed to be catching a cold.)

A slight pause then, and then, very faintly and sadly, she sang a paraphrase of an old song, giving it dreadful words. *There'll be a hot time in Lakehurst, New Jersey, when the* Hindenburg *lands tonight. . . .*

"Moise, come to the window and look at the candleglow on the frost, it's a metaphor, too."

Her reply was a choking sound. I whirled to face her and saw that now she *had* gone into a seizure. I snatched up the wooden spatula to depress her tongue. Her eyes circled like gray pinwheels for a few moments: then rose halfway under her upper eyelids as her twitching and salivating lips uttered an unconscious and long-drawn "*Ahhh*," and I knew then that she'd gone into sleep for a while. I touched her small, lovely breast to make sure that it was moving with breath. Then I used the interlude of her slumber to set things straight in the Blue Jay.

About Moise's tirade, I had mixed feelings. I didn't doubt it was meant, since followed by the seizure and her breaths of exhaustion, but still it struck me somewhat as a

184

theater curtain does after a climactic explosion of speeches. Spurious, no, but a thing that is set and built up to.

I was writing it down with all reasonable accuracy when she came out of her sleep and in a faint and faraway voice said to me, "Well, what happened, did I blow it?"

"Well, frankly"

"What?"

"If you mean your cool, I would say yes."

"Well, I feel much better after my"

"Hour of?"

"Oblivion to Mother, Moppet, and all scavenger crones, oh, if only I had equipment for painting. The pigments and the canvas are my *milieu,* not the words and the impossible telling of things. You know, if blood weren't red and my palette cool color, I'd cut your throat and finger-paint with your blood on the walls of the room."

"Moise, you are a savage."

"So are you and all the honest remaining"

"Nothing will be published and nothing will be painted anymore now in the future."

"Right as rain in dry country."

"Let's face it frontally, not with"

"Prevaricating backsides. Agreed, *d'accord,* but—"

Whatever qualification she was about to mention was interrupted by a loud thump outside the door on Bleecker. She seemed not to hear it. . . . However, I did, clearly, and had the courage to get up and run down the long, long, shuddering corridor to . . .

◆

The thumping sound at the door was that of an act of divine providence occurring in the form of a great package delivered outside Moise's door, and it was an act so divinely providential that I think it justifies my frequent allusions to God in the course of this writing and even concluding this sentence with that debased form of punctuation the exclamation point, but having referred to that mark I can spare myself the use of it.

Of course I don't mean to confuse you. The act of divine providence, the delivery at the door of Moise, was a collaborative act, or actions, by the living Actress Invicta and Tony Smith of Hunter and South Orange with possibly Celebrity Service involved as

Intermediary or entrepreneur, you name it, but anyway the Actress Invicta has been phenomenally quick in delivering the appeal to the Smiths in South Orange, considering her whirlwind involvement in the social life of upper-class Manhattan and her emotional involvement in tracking down Big Lot.

Implements of painting have been delivered by the discreetly hastily departing deliverer of them, no running footsteps heard or motor starting. There is a carefully chosen number of tubes of paint, brushes for bold strokes and for delicate touches and various sizes of stretched canvas, a tube of Perma-Gel, large bottles of linseed and turp, a casserole dish of shrimp curry, and along with all this a note in an irregular hand to the effect that when stores are opened, a supply of tinned goods will be ordered for deposit at Moise's door each Monday, until she is prepared to submit herself to the strain of a small exhibition at Hunter with guests of discriminate selection.

It was evident that the Actress Invicta had mentioned the hissing incident of Skates, there was a postscript that read, "If Skates should crash the exhibit, the tongue with which she hisses will be torn out with hot pincers."

It was almost immediately after this event that Moise had another seizure and I depressed her tongue again with the dingy wooden spatula by the bed.

She came out of it with a sigh and a smile and one of those oracular or visionary utterances for whose recording I had kept a Blue Jay here.

"I am deeply saddened by the necessity of declining their invitation to join the Symbionese Liberation Army as their Field Marshal's mate. Please contact them for me and explain that the flattering offer has arrived a day late but that I hope that God and time will permit me to use new pigments and brushes from South Orange, New Jersey, to attempt a canvas which they can use as an anarchistic emblem, provided my inescapably oblique style of work is not insufficiently forceful. Oh, but say I must wait till I have forgotten their emblem of serpents, having lately"

Her breath expired at this point but the reference to serpents and to lately made me aware that, after all, she had not been oblivious to Skates's performance the evening before.

As for her knowing of the Symbionese Liberation Army and its Field Marshal, all I can say is that madness is visionary, since she no longer permits any kind or article of mass media to come into her room.

··•

Just now she has interrupted this entry into the Blue Jay by approaching me on her bare knees with a damp rag and has addressed me as *"mon petit capitain"* (presumably of the S.L.A.) and has begun to bathe my bare feet in warm water. And now she is bending to dry them with her long hair let down.

I had to take a firm hand.

"Stop this foolishness, dear, and get to work on your anarchistic banner."

"Yes, *mon petit capitain*," she whispered.

I helped her to her feet and then she made a gesture toward a canvas on an easel and, to my astonishment, there was the beginning of her work on a design for the emblem to replace the snakes, in her "oblique" style but with touches of orange and pink and red.

It had already the oblique suggestion of an artist committed to a spirit of revolution but waiting for God and time.

I am back into the Blue Jay but aware that Moise has admitted the pair of men with the box cameras to the room and in their dark and beautifully tailored mohairs they are moving about to photograph her new canvas in its initial stage. The room is full of faint whispers and equally faint clickings and outside is also a faint sound of Jack Frost dissolving his etching on the window through which comes the faintness of late winter afternoon light.

A glimmer of light refracted from the remarkably large crystal lens of a box camera has made me lift my eyes, and now once again I have to record a bizarre distraction and one of such an agreeable nature that I suspect that I will not continue this day's work much longer.

When I looked up I observed that the younger of the two men with the fantastic box cameras was looking directly at me, his eyes containing a very blue and open declaration of love. Naturally I returned it, it would have been completely impossible not to. But he is apparently shy and the instant that I answered his look of love with my own he turned his back to me and I observed a very interesting thing. He had removed his jacket and I observed that his shoulders are twice the breadth of his hips and that the silky dark mohair of his trouser-legs adheres to his upper thighs as closely as paint to canvas and I also observed that his hair is not prematurely white but a very pale natural gold.

It will soon be dark in the room and I wonder if the boldness that makes my heart skip a beat will somehow manage to exorcise his timidity, his Northern but elegant restraint, and whether or not in answer to that question, to me a question of almost suffocating excitement, three more faint sounds in close but not hurried succession are heard in the world of Moise: the click of a box with a square crystal eye, a click of frost on the window, and from Moise a whisper.

"I do believe we all belong in this room."

"Thank you, yes," said the man who'd removed his jacket and folded it neatly as a jacket at the Brothers Brooks and placed it beside her tealess tea things on the box next to her bed.

"Not me but God," said Moise in a tone that might be described as one of ineffable sweetness, phrase by courtesy of countless Victorian pen-pushers.

She drew a breath and continued, "I think He knows that the violence of reason must wait upon the soft anneal-ments of love, at least till"

She did not complete this whisper, and, looking up again, I could see why she didn't. It was a case of turning from expression to action. She had crawled on her knees to the cameraman who still had on his jacket and with her delicate artist's fingers she was removing his trousers. To be more exact about it, she was loosening the waistband of his trousers while her other hand reached behind her beneath her surprisingly wide bed and drew from beneath it a jar that contained a bit of petroleum jelly, which divine providence would soon replace with a full one.

Of course I diverted my eyes from the ecstasy of Moise to the object of my own, yes, indeed, to the jacketless cameraman, and I observed that he was now standing in tall profile to me, his back to Moise and his partner.

This position in profile, the tallness of it with delicate gleams here and there, almost broke my heart, but he repaired this almost-heartbreak with a very slight up and down motion of his head which I have chosen to mean a soundless assent, like that of a timid bride, before a marriage altar.

It isn't yet dark in the room but dim and dimmer and all that I hear now are the footsteps of a giant being, as hushed as they are gigantic, footsteps of the Great Unknown One approaching our world of reason or unreason, you name it as you conceive it. And now

The last Blue Jay is completed.